4 Head kissers
Short Erotic Tales

Monáe Jae

Printed in the United States of America

First printing, 2015

Cover Image By: Eshama J Photography
Cover Model Male: John Doe
Cover Model Female: Monae Jae

ISBN 978-0-9965053-2-1

4 Head Kissers Short Erotic Tales

WWW.4headkissers.com

I would first like to say glory be to God, without him I'am nothing. Thank you God for guiding me, and never leaving me even at my darkest hour. Thank you for my gift of writing. Thank you lord for keeping me focused. I'am forever humbled, and grateful for your mercy, and all your many blessings. Thank you for making all of this possible.

God is Good Everyday B.

For my cooking up a storm, crazy, sexy, caring, big mouth Aunt Cherl (Sexy Blonde Bitch) May you sleep in peace Cheryl Lee Bartee. You are forever in my heart.

Shout outs to my Ex! I know he screaming fuck me, so shout outs to the sex!

ARE YOU A 4 HEAD KISSER?

Are You A 4 Head Kisser?

CHAPTER ONE

Baltimore Terrace

Trista sat at home on her couch on a Friday night, flipping through the same Channels on television over and over again. She had already watched all the DVDs she owned. She'd even watched the movies that were on demand. This was sad. Here she was 24 years old in the house on a Friday night alone. All her friends were either hooked up or miles away.

She hadn't had sex since her last boyfriend and that was over five months ago. Trista could have easily hit him up to go a few rounds. But she refused to let his cheating ass get any of her good stuff. Secondly she damn sure wasn't going to let him think she was desperate and couldn't find better after him. She thought about taking a cold shower, or even a hot one with one of her toys.

Trista quickly decided against that. She needed real penetration and her toys were no longer cutting it. She let out a deep sigh, as she continued to flip through channels. Maybe calling Marcus up wasn't as desperate as it sounded. Trista quickly dismissed the thought for a second time, for the same reasons as the first. She decided to go sit out on her terrace.

Trista went into her kitchen and opened a bottle of wine. She poured herself a glass and then put the bottle back in place. Halfway to the terrace she had already finished that glass. Trista went turned back to retrieve the entire bottle. She then walked back into the living room and slid the sliding doors open.

Trista peeked her head through the door before walking out on to the terrace. Right away she was hit with a nice summer breeze. The terrace was pitch black. The only light she had was from her television that still played on without her. There was also the light from the city of Baltimore shining below her.

She leaned over, and looked down on the city. *It looked so pretty at night*, she thought. Trista picked the bottle of wine up, bringing it up to her lips, drinking straight from the bottle, and staring in to space. *Everything looked so tiny from the 24th floor.* She raised the bottle to her lips again, when out the corner of the darkness she heard a deep baritone voice say, "long week huh?" Trista jumped abruptly. The glass she held in her hand slipped over the metal railing. She put her hand to her chest and peered into the darkness. "Who's there?" She called out.

She couldn't see anything. Out the corner of her eye she saw the light from the end of what smelled like a cigar. "I'm over here… Sorry I startled you," said the voice. Trista was vexed. "Well it's too damn late for sorry! My got damn glass is already long gone!" Trista snarled. The dark figure now moved closer to their own terrace ledge and looked down. "Yeah I guess you're right. Sorry about that again." Trista could now see his face.

He was well shaven, about 6'3, nicely built. He looked as if he hit the gym two to three times a week. He had small chinky eyes, nice thick eyebrows, sexy full lips, and a cute nose. *Who the hell was he?* Trista thought. *She had never seen this man before in her entire two years of living in the building. Then again I didn't really know anyone in the whole building. Besides the doorman, the janitor, and the mail lady. Trista wasn't even sure if the mail lady should even be considered.*

Trista cut her thoughts short and focused her attention back on the stranger. He sure was fine. Trista took another swig from the bottle of wine, but kept her eyes fixed on him. "You must have had a long week huh?" Asked the stranger. " And, how did you come to that conclusion?" Trista asked sounding slightly annoyed.

 The stranger took another pull from his cigar before speaking. "Well for starters you're drinking straight from the bottle, secondly it's Friday, and lastly you look like a pretty young lady. You should be out shaking something, yet you're in the quietness of your home." He slowly walked back over to the corner from which he emerged from, and sat down on a small chair. If it were not for the end of his cigar, and his white tank top, Trista would not have known he was still there.

Trista took a step back, crossing her arms in the process. "Well for your information this is my damn bottle of wine, so I can do what I please with it! Secondly I had a glass until some maniac emerged from the darkness, creeping up on me, scaring me half to death! Lastly Mr. creep! Not every young female likes to go out every Friday, Saturday, Sunday, to shake her ass on, or in front of someone!" With that being said Trista stormed off the terrace slamming the sliding door behind her.

She was pissed. "The nerve of that damn guy. He doesn't even know me like that to be all up in my business! Or even sneaking up on me the way he did! Creep!" She said aloud, as she plopped down on her queen size mattress. "Shit!" She cursed herself. She was in need of another glass of wine, but because she left so abruptly she'd forgotten to take the bottle with her. Trista sucked her teeth.

She was not about to go back out there after she had just told him off. Plus not to mention leaving the way she did. If she went back out there she would make a complete fool of herself. She let out a deep sigh as she looked over at the clock on her nightstand. The clock read 12 am. Trista's eyes then fell on her laundry basket, which was on the opposite side of her master bedroom; it was over flowing with dirty clothes. She decided to sort them. After she had sorted them, she decided to take them down to the laundry room.

This was no big deal, because the laundry room was located in the basement of her building. It's not like she was going to fall asleep anytime soon, and she didn't have anything or anyone to aid her with that, so this laundry would definitely have to do the trick. She took off the clothes she was wearing and threw them in with the other clothes, and then headed to the bathroom to take a quick shower before putting everything in to her pushcart. On her way out she grabbed her keys, mace, and tablet, so she could listen to music and read while she waited. As she was unlocking her front door she heard a knock at it.

Trista thought she was going crazy. She peeked through the peephole and there this anonymous creep stood. *He must have not gotten enough of her telling him off.* She unlocked the door but kept the chain on. "What can I do for you? Mr. creep up on people in the middle of the night! You have some more assumptions for me huh?" Trista was still pissed and she was letting it be known.

"Well actually no... I have no assumptions. I don't want any trouble. I just came over here to apologize properly. I really didn't mean to assume or offend you." "Well you did!" Snapped Trista. "Well I really didn't mean too. Look we got off on the wrong foot. I should have properly introduced myself. I was busy being such a creep!" He said jokingly, using Trista choice of words. " Hello I'm Elias." He extended his hand.

Trista closed the door removed the chain, and then opened the door fully. She immediately got a whiff of his cologne. *Good goodness he smelt good. There was always something about a man that smelt good that made them more attractive in her eyes. His features looked so much better up close. He was not 6'3, but in fact 6'4. His skin was an almond complexion, it looked very smooth, and flawless. His small chinky eyes were even more seductive in person.*

"Are you going to shake my hand, or are you going to let it go numb?" Trista snapped out of her gaze. "Oh of course." She said feeling just a little embarrassed. She reached out and shook his hand, which was the opposite of what she was expecting. Trista figured he would have rough hands being that he was nicely built. She assumed he did some sort of construction, or some other sort of hands on labor that would require some type of strength.

She quickly pulled her hand from his grip. She opened her door wider and backed her cart out into the hallway. "Laundry this late?" Elias looked a bit confused. "Yes do you mind? Last time I checked there was no laws passed on how late you could wash your clothing!" Elias shook his head. "Oh not at all. Its just late that's all and you're by yourself. That isn't very safe." "Well I always go around this time no one is ever up. There's nothing but a bunch of old retired folks living in this building anyways; so I think I'll take my chances. She flashed her mace at him, which was attached to her keys. Then she turned to lock up her apartment.

" Okay if you say so little lady. Nice meeting you." He smiled and then walked back across the hallway to his apartment. Trista called for the elevator. Once it arrived she backed her pushcart on it. She rode it all the way down. She couldn't help but think about how attractive that guy was up in person. It was still a bit strange that she had never seen him before. Being that she had been living in the building almost two years now.

The elevator doors opened and she walked out into the poorly lit basement. It did look a bit scary being down here by yourself, however it was furnished nicely, and for a basement it was real clean. There were about a dozen dryers, another dozen washers, a few baskets, and some carts with wheels. There was also a flat screen television mounted to a wall. A cute little sofa and a large folding table sat in the middle of the floor.

Trista decided to listen to Internet radio. She put her headphones in, as she began putting stuff into the washers. First she put in her colored clothes, then whites. An old song by the group Troop came on. Trista turned the volume on her headphones all the way up. "This is my song," She sang the lyrics aloud as she poured detergent into her loads. Trista felt as if she was being watched, but before she could turn around to make sure she was still alone. A figure reached out and snatched one of her headphones out of her ear.

There he was again. The strange guy. Trista jumped back, holding her hands up to her chest. "Little lady you must be trying to get yourself hurt blasting your music this loud. I could have been a crazy person out to get you, and you wouldn't have even seen it coming." He flashed a perfect white smile. He then held up a bottle of wine and two wine glasses in front of her face. "You just love creeping up on people don't you?" Trista slammed the bottle of detergent down and crossed her arms in front of her chest.

"Well actually this time I honestly wasn't trying too. I called out to you several times." "Oh… well I didn't hear you." He laughed, "I know. I thought you could use some company so I brought down the little bit of laundry I had, a bottle of wine, and a replacement glass for the one I helped you break earlier." Trista smiled, *so he wasn't that much of a creep after all.* She thought to herself, as he peered down at her.

"Oh my gosh! Wow she smiles!" Elias said sarcastically. He was happy to see that Trista wasn't one of those stuck up types who couldn't take a joke, or have any fun. He sat the wine bottle and glasses on top of a near by washing machine. Elias then went back over to the entrance to where he left his laundry bag sitting. " Do you mind helping a guy figure this out?" He held his laundry bag up in front of Trista with a pitiful look on his face.

Trista busted out with laughter. "Wait a minute!" She said holding one hands in the air. "You mean to tell me you don't know how to do your own laundry?" "Dang girl could you be any louder." Elias said jokingly holding his finger up to his lips. "I mean I do know. I'm just not good at it, at all. I usually take everything down to the drop off service." Trista pondered to herself for a second before responding. "Okay I'll help you, but just this once. Only because you brought down more wine and I could use the company. This basement is a bit scary when you're down here alone. That goes for male or female."

Elias quickly looked around. "You ain't never lie," they both laughed. Once Trista started up his loads she took a seat on top of one of the machines, so she could be at eye level with him. Elias leaned back against one of the folding tables and poured them both a glass of wine. He raised his glass to propose a toast. "To..." " Trista immediately cut him off "To no more creeping," They both cried out with laughter again. "Yeah to no more creeping," They touched glasses.

"So how come I've never seen you around?" Trista went straight into grilling him for information about himself. "Well maybe because I'm in the process of moving out, so I'm never really here. I just sleep here on the nights I'm in town." "Oh ok. Well how come you're moving?" "I own my own insurance company. We are in the process of relocating to another part of Baltimore, so I need to be closer to our corporate office."

"Oh okay." Said Trista flatly. "That's all you have to say is oh okay?" He chuckled before finishing his glass of wine. "Yeah I mean... don't take this the wrong way, but you don't strike me as the own your own business kind of guy." Elias chuckled at her response. " Oh no and why is that?" He poured them both another glass eager to hear her answer.

Trista threw back her second glass before speaking. "I

just didn't! You look like you would be into construction, or fitness, or something like that." He laughed, "Damn. Okay I see, so you mean to tell me a brother can't look good and own his own business." They both laughed aloud again. "So what about you little lady? What do you do for a living?" "I'm a lawyer." Trista said firmly with her head held proudly.

" Oh so that explains why you jumped down my damn throat earlier on the terrace." She laughed at his sly remark. "No! I told you about yourself, because you scared me half to death and secondly." "That's right Ms. lawyer state your case." Elias said cutting her off in mid rant. He flashed a smile causing Trista to smile once more. "Okay so maybe I' am a bit defensive." " It's ok I like that." Elias said looking right at her.

They both stared at each other and before she knew it he was standing in between her legs. Trista's heart began to race. Her skin started to get clammy, as if somebody turned up the heat. "You are very beautiful also. I like that too." Their eyes never left each others as he spoke. Elias put one hand on her waist, as he pulled her closer to the edge of the washer. He took his other hand and massaged her inner thigh.

Trista's mind was racing. *What the hell did this guy think he was doing? He needed to stop. But a part of her couldn't get the nerve up to stop him. Truth be told she didn't want him to stop. He was so enticing and sexy.* Trista let him take one leg out of her shorts. He then started planting wet kisses on her inner thighs, while massaging her clitoris through her panties.

Elias pulled them to the side and kissed her vagina lips. He followed up by licking them. Trista clutched on to both his shoulders, basically daring him to go further. Elias took

14

one leg out of her panties, and then spread her vagina lips again with his tongue. He went in and out slowly with his tongue, fastening his pace a bit. Trista was now griping the back of his neck, while grinding her kitty cat against his thick tongue and full lips.

She was about to climax. She needed this. *I need this.* That's all her inner thoughts were repeating to her. It had been so long since she had her pussy eaten this good. She held her head back and moaned. Elias was getting the job done. Trista could care less that just an hour ago she thought he was some creep. She held on even tighter just as the washer went into spin cycle.

Elias kept licking and sucking. He had not one care in the world, savoring the taste of Trista's juices on his tongue each time he licked her. He was on a mission to get Trista to climax like she had never before, judging by how tight she gripped the back of his neck he knew he was getting the job done. All of a sudden the wine glass she had sat on the washer went crashing to the floor, interrupting what they were doing. "Shit!" Trista said aloud.

Elias backed up a bit with caution so not to step on the broken pieces of glass. "Seems like you and wine glasses don't get along." He said grinning, and then licking his lips. All of a sudden Trista felt embarrassed. She looked down at herself. Her panties and shorts were hanging on to the end of her right leg. Her bare ass was sitting up on some nasty public washing machine, letting a stranger eat her out. Trista put her leg back through her clothing and jumped down.

"This is awkward." Said Elias. He scratched the back of his head and looked away. "Yes it is!" Trista said, while quickly gathering her wet clothes out of the washer and throwing them into her laundry bags and cart. " Wait you don't have to go! I'm sorry I shouldn't have gotten carried away, its just that you are so." Trista cut him off. "No really it's not your fault. I shouldn't have let you get carried away." She grabbed her cart and belongings.

Trista hurried towards the elevator. when she heard Elias running for the elevator she smashed the button so that the doors would close. Trista cursed herself. *What the hell was she thinking going there with a stranger?* The elevator doors opened up on her floor . Trista quickly ran to her apartment door and went in. She immediately locked the door behind her. She stayed there momentarily trying to catch her breath.

She was in need of another shower. Trista headed straight for the bathroom. She was only in there about three minutes or so. Moments later Trista heard heavy knocks at her front door. Trista already knew who it was. She took a deep breath. She was not ready to stand face to face with Elias again. She quickly rinsed off as much suds as she could, then grabbed her thick hooded robe. She slipped it on as she walked towards the door, speaking loud enough for Elias to hear on the other side.

"Go away Elias! I don't want to talk right now!" She yelled at him with her back to the door. "I'm not leaving until you talk to me!" Elias knocked on the door again. "Fuck! He's going to wake up the other tenants." Trista tied her robe tightly before opening the door a little. She stuck her head out and whispered to him "That wasn't suppose to happen. Matter of fact lets pretend it didn't happen! And now you have to go." She tried to close the door, but Elias put his foot between it. His tone was hushed as well.

"But it did happen Trista. In fact I think you wanted it to happen. Hell I wanted it to happen too. What's wrong with that Trista?" Trista lowered her head a bit. "Nothing, but I just… I just met you and…" "So and what?" Elias reached in and kissed her. He pushed her back into her apartment, letting the door slam behind them. She kissed him back wildly and passionately. She lifted his shirt up over his head.

Elias loosed the straps on her robe before picking her up. Trista wrapped her legs around his waist and back. Still engaged in their kiss Elias struggled to see where everything was in the dark. He couldn't make out a thing, but he could see the lights gleaming from the city below out on the terrace. He inched closer to the Terrace and slid the door open.

The air felt good against Trista's bathed skin. Elias pinned her up against the small chaise. He began to kiss her neck and shoulders. Elias took one of her breast into his mouth, gently sucking on it. Trista undid his sweat pants and let them fall to his ankles. Elias's hard dick needed no waking up. All ten inches of it laid there, curving slightly to the right. Trista could see this through his briefs. She ran her hands over it, caressing it as he continued to suck her breast.

Trista tugged at his boxers a few moments. When she was unable to get them down, she gave up. Elias smiled down at her, and then took a step back. He stepped out of the remainder of his clothing. His body looked amazing. Trista squinted some to get a better look at his penis. He had one of those dicks that you just wanted to suck. It looked so good. Elias's dick was thick and long just the way she liked.. Trista pulled him closer to her. She took him into her mouth as much as she could. She licked and sucked the shaft of his dick, while jerking it.

Elias put his hand behind her head, guiding her up and down as she sucked. He let her continue for a few moments before pulling her away. Elias didn't want to cum just yet. "Stand up and turn around. I want to taste your sweet pussy one more time." Trista got up and did as she was told. She turned around and put one leg up on the chaise. Elias got down on one knee and began to suck her pussy lips.

He parted them with his tongue and then slid it in. He maneuvered his tongue around her pussy walls, making sure nothing was left unsatisfied. Trista gripped his shoulders as she began to moan aloud. "Yes! Yes! Yes that's it. Make this pussy wet for you! Make this pussy cum for you." Trista's leg began to shake. She tried to push Elias's face from in between her legs, but he gripped her thighs holding her in place. He stuck his tongue in and out, deeper and faster until she had no choice but to climax.

Trista stood there in complete bliss soaking up her orgasm, but her moment was cut short. Elias stood up and gripped her waist. He pushed her slightly, forcing her to bend over the terrace. He pulled her robe up and gripped her ass cheeks. He then made Trista spread her legs. He reached in and fingered her. Elias wanted to make sure she was still wet and ready for him to enter her. Elias smacked his dick against her pussy lips. He then slid it inside of Trista slowly. "Arch your back." He whispered into her ear.

Trista arched her back as much as she could. Elias

stroked his dick in and out of her hard and fast. "Let me see you throw your ass back on this dick." He mumbled. Without any hesitation Trista bounced her ass back causing it to slap against his mid section. Trista allowed her mind and body to completely relax. She let go of all the negative thoughts bombarding her head. She allowed Elias to take her to ecstasy; a feeling her body so desperately needed.

She tuned everything out. The only sound she could hear were the sounds of her own heavy breathing, the squirting noises her pussy made each time Elias pushed his hard dick inside of her. " Yeah baby just like that cum on this dick." Elias reached down and gripped a handful of Trista's hair, while he held on to her waist with his other hand. Elias pumped in and out of her. Each time he pulled back he made sure to push his entire dick into her.

Trista was now moaning loudly as though she couldn't handle it, but she wasn't running, she continued to meet his every thrust. The head of his dick was hitting her walls in such a way that Trista's legs began to shake again. "I'm about to cum! I'm about to cum!" She exclaimed at the top of her lungs. "That's what I want you to do. Cum for me baby. Cum on this dick." Elias gripped her ass cheeks, as he let out one last stroke before they both stopped moving. Their bodies stayed there in the same position. Elias leaning over Trista, while her juices oozed out. Both of their naked bodies leaning over the ledge, looking down on the city of Baltimore.

CHAPTER TWO

Milking It

Tessa looked down at her watch. She had been stuck in traffic for well over thirty Minutes now. She was about to be late for an extremely important business meeting. Tessa glanced over at the meter in the cab. It was now at about forty dollars, and she wasn't even within 10 blocks from where she needed to be. The light changed green for the second time, yet they did not move a damn inch.

Tessa's thoughts raced back and forth. *I might as well get out and crawl to my destination. I'd put my last on it, that I would make it there before the cab did*. Tessa slammed her hand down on top of a folder of paper work, which sat on of her briefcase beside her. "Why today of all days?" She exclaimed. She looked out the window. In the next lane there was a little boy with his face stuck to the car window, staring directly at her. When she stared back he stuck his tongue out at her.

Tessa frowned and looked back at her watch. Her eyes then glanced at the meter again. She quickly got the cab drivers attention by tapping on the back of the driver seat.

"Sir can you let me out right here please!" The cab driver stopped the meter. Tessa handed him a fifty-dollar bill. She looked around the backseat, grabbed her brief case, paper work, and exited the cab. Tessa crossed the street and headed towards the train station.

She hurried down the flight of stairs. She hadn't taken the subway in so long. She didn't even know how much the fare was. Tessa walked up to a booth. A man sat behind it. He talked in a thick Jamaican accent as he rudely directed her towards a machine. Once at the machine she purchased a single ride train ticket. Tessa ran towards the turnstile. The train she needed was approaching the station. Tessa boarded the train. She didn't even bother to sit down. There was no point. She was only going two stops.

She still had about 15 minutes to make her meeting on time. She looked down at her watch for like the 100th time. "Gosh!" She tapped her foot impatiently waiting for the train doors to close. Tessa hated rushing. This was her main reason for leaving her place early. Ironically she still was running late. "Oh the fucking joys of living in the city." She mumbled. Two stops later the doors opened. Tessa ran out towards the flight of stairs. She still had about ten minutes. She looked down at her watch and continued to run. Suddenly she felt herself falling. Before Tessa could stop herself she collided with some asshole.

Her briefcase hit the ground and her paper work went flying into the air. People around them scrambled to help pick them up. The stranger immediately reached out his hand to help her up. She stubbornly took his hand, and used his body as an aid to pick herself up. "Are you okay ma'am?" He asked "politely. "I'm fine!" Tessa said, while snatching her hand back and then smoothing out her suit. She took her now wrinkled up paper work from his hands. She picked up her briefcase, and continued on her way.

Tessa had no time to be mad, dwell, or even make sure she didn't forget anything. All she had was seven minutes. Exactly seven minutes to get up to her office, check her hair makeup, and then sell these people her Idea...

Tessa opened the door to her condo. She wanted nothing more than a drink. Today had been beyond rough. She didn't even bother to go to her bedroom to change. Tessa sat her briefcase down on the floor, kicked off her shoes, and stripped down right at the front door. She headed straight for her bar. She crossed her living room floor, and took a seat at her little bar area. Tessa skipped over the bottles of wine and grabbed a bottle of vodka.

She poured herself a shot. "Here's to this sucky ass day!" She said aloud. She then took the drink straight to the head, and then immediately poured another. "And here's to the million dollar deal I closed in spite of it. Tessa threw the shot back just as she did the first. She was about to pour another shot, when she heard a knock at her front door. She looked at her watch. It read 7pm. *She wasn't expecting any damn company. The doorman damn sure didn't notify her that anyone was coming up, so who the hell was at her door?* She got up to see. "Who is it?" she snapped, as if whoever it was could hear her through the steel door.

She unlocked the door and snatched it open. You would think she would be a bit embarrassed that she was standing there in her bra and garter pantyhose, but she was far from it. Instead she was pissed to see it was the same asshole she had collided into earlier in the subway.

22

"What the hell are you doing here?" Tessa said folding her arms and turning up her nose at him. He immediately reached into his bag, pulling out a few wrinkled papers.

"Sorry to disturb you… It's just that you ran away so quickly I couldn't give them to you. I didn't know how important they were to you, so I looked you up. I hope you don't mind." He handed the papers over to her. Tessa reached out and snatched them from his hands. "Thanks a lot you clumsy fuck!" She snarled at him and then slammed her door in his face. "Damn! That was really harsh."

Tessa took a sip from the bottle of liquor she held in her hand. She rolled her eyes, and then turned around to open the front door back up. "Hey hold on a second!" She called out after the stranger. "Oh I'm sorry are you talking to this clumsy fuck?" The Stranger said sarcastically. Tessa stepped out the door a little more. "I'm sorry. You really didn't deserve that… Look my day has been pure mayhem… do forgive my rudeness. Come back and have a drink. It's on me." Tessa motioned with her hand for him to come back.

" You know… I think I really should get going." He looked down at his watch. "Why? Are you married?" He laughed. "No I'm not married." "Okay then! Don't be such a pussy! Come have a drink with me." She walked back into her apartment leaving the door open behind her. This time she sashayed back over to the bar, trying to deciding if she should stand behind it instead of taking a seat.

Moments later the stranger entered the apartment slowly. He adjusted his eyes to the dim lighting inside. "I'm in here." Tessa called out to him. He followed the sound of her voice. "Watch your..." It was too late. He had already tripped on the two steps, that you had to step up, in order to enter the living room area. He stumbled a bit, but caught his balance. Tessa laughed. "I'm Sorry I tried to warn you." She said covering her mouth.

He smiled awkwardly as he looked around. "Nice place you have here." "Why thank you. Here have a seat." She pointed at one of the bars stools. He sat his briefcase down on the floor and took a seat at the stool. "So what can I get you? Matter of fact let me guess." She looked him over once with her eyes. "You look like a Scotch man." He laughed. "Am I correct?" Tessa looked at him with one eyebrow raised.

"Yes… Yes you are. How'd you know?" Tessa turned to make his drink "I use to bartend while in college to help put myself through school. So believe me when I tell you I know a scotch man when I see one." She sat his drink in front of him. He sipped slowly, while looking around in amazement, but also seemed a bit nervous. Tessa automatically read his expressions and vibe.

She cleared her throat. "Don't worry. I don't have a boyfriend, and there's no boogeyman under the couch or in the closet, waiting to jump out and get you." He laughed again. "So you were a psychic once too in college too?" He said with his voice dripping with sarcasm. "No! I'm just good at reading people." She said flatly. "Oh really?" "Yes really!" Tessa snapped. He started to laugh again. "Oh so you want to try me? Ask me something I don't know about you. Anything!" Tessa dared him.

He stopped sipping his drink and sat up straight. "Okay since you insist. What is it you think I do for a living?" Tessa stepped back and examined him. "That's too easy!

24

Next question." Tessa said. He laughed again. "No please tell me." Tessa sucked her teeth before speaking. "Well judging by your pager and your choice of sneakers with a suit. I take it your some kind of doctor. Only doctors carry pagers these days. You probably had just as long of a day as I, and because of it you needed to change your shoes."

He ran his hands through his hair and smiled. "Okay, so maybe that was easy. Next question. What do you think I'm thinking about now?" Tessa smirked, and raised her eyebrow once more. "See now that's a question I like." She licked her lips before answering. "Well judging by the way you keep looking at my body you are definitely attracted to me. Oh and…" She leaned in close to him, so close her nose was almost touching his, causing him to turn red slightly.

"You could use another drink." Tessa whispered as she grabbed his glass. The stranger knew his face had to be a bright red by now, but he managed to laugh it off. "Okay, so you're really really good." He took his second drink from her hand. "Can you guess what I'm thinking?" Asked Tessa, jumping right back into things. He chuckled. "Unfortunately I'm not as good at reading people, or their minds as you are."

Tessa grinned. "Okay, so why don't I just tell you then! I'm thinking how long is it going to take you to finish that drink, come around this bar counter, and fuck the shit out of me?" He covered his mouth quickly to stop his drink from escaping his lips. He coughed uncontrollably, as an attempt to prevent himself from choking on his own Saliva. Tessa stared at him unmoved. She spoke up, "But if you're not man enough to handle that I understand." She walked around the bar counter towards the front door.

He reached out and grabbed her arm, stopping her in place. "Wait a minute! May I please have another?" Tessa's eyes shifted from his hand on her arm to his hair, then back to the glass that sat in front of him. She shook free of his grasp and picked up the glass. She walked back around the bar counter. He began to loosen his tie, and then he ran his fingers through his blonde hair once more. "You know I've never done anything like this before."

He didn't get the chance to utter another word. Because Tessa turned around and slammed his drink on the bar top, Causing some of it to spill a little. She grabbed his tie and pulled him to her lips. She kissed him, as if she craved his very being. She then climbed on top of the bar top and sat with her legs open in front of him. She yanked his tie indicating to him that she wanted him on his feet.

Tessa sucked and kissed his neck, leaving red marks all over it. She undid his shirt, and then proceeded to undo his pants. But he abruptly reached down, and gabbed her hands. "Maybe we shouldn't…" Before another word could exit his lips, Tessa hauled off and slapped the shit out of him. "Maybe we shouldn't do what?" She asked. She gripped the back of his neck and kissed him roughly. This time his passion matched hers.

He pulled the straps to her bra down. Tessa's hard nipples stood at full attention. He wanted to take them into his mouth right then and there. Instead he lifted her body up off the bar top, while squeezing her butt cheeks through her pantyhose. He put her down and forced her to lean over one of the stools, letting his pants and briefs drop down to his ankles in the process. He couldn't figure out how to unhook the garter, so he ripped her right out of it.

Without hesitation he grabbed her hair, and pushed his hard dick inside of her. Never had he felt a rush like this before. He pumped in and out of her slowly. Tessa's pussy juices felt so good on his dick. The feeling was so good he started to drool slightly. He wanted nothing more than to soak in it. "Stop being a pussy! And fuck me. Fuck me hard!" Tessa moaned out.

He grabbed both her shoulders, and pushed her back on to his manhood. He slammed into her as hard as he could. "Yes just like that! Make this pussy wet for you. Let this pussy feel you!" He continued to stroke in and out of her, letting her juices flow from inside her down the inside of her thighs. He flipped her back around, making her lay across two of the bar stools. He grabbed her thighs and slid her to the edged, and then he dipped just the head of his dick in and out of her, teasing her a bit. Each time he did this Tessa clenched her pussy muscles as tight as she could.

"Fuck me just like that!" She moaned, and purred aloud, dragging each word that left her lips. Without warning he pushed deep inside of her. He bent his knees slightly and gripped her inner thighs. Tessa reached up, and grabbed the tie that was still around his neck. She pulled him close to her. His skin up against hers looked like milk when mixed with coffee. Tessa stared directly into his green eyes.

"What's your name?" She whispered into his ear. "Chase! Chase! My name is Chase!" His words barely made it from his lips. "Chase I'm about to cum. Fuck this pussy Chase like you want it to cum! You want me to cum on your dick don't you Chase?" Chase shook his head yes, while his mouth hung wide open. Chase pushed deeper inside of her until he felt her body start to tremor.

Tessa dug her nails into the back of his neck as she climaxed. Once Chase felt her release all over him, he then let out one last hard stroke. Without warning his legs gave in on him, and he collapsed to his knees.

CHAPTER THREE

Bipolar

"Quit playing! Stop! No for real sssstop!" Kenya begged and stuttered, as Kahless kissed, and climbed on top of her, sucking on her neck. *Was this really happening?* Kenya couldn't separate what her mind wanted from what her body was saying she wanted. To make matters worse. Kahless really wasn't concerned about what neither one was saying. Kahless was in another place.

She was in the clouds, and intoxicated from the drinks she had consumed not too long ago. Truth is she was physically attracted to Kenya and vise versa. It's just that everything was happening too fast. The two of them went from talking about their jobs, guys, and problems, to taking shots of vodka, to kissing. Now here they were dry humping each other. Kahless was aroused and she wasn't trying to take no for an answer.

Kenya on the other hand just couldn't allow this to happen. The both of them had boyfriends. Honestly their boyfriends probably wouldn't even care about what was taking place, but Kenya did. She always told herself that if she'd ever slept with a female, then that female would have to be drop dead gorgeous. So gorgeous that no one would even question her change in preference.

Not to say that Kahless wasn't bad in her own right. She was indeed sexy as shit and very seductive. Kahless had a nice Carmel complexion, thick thighs, hips, and an ass to match. Plus she looked good in just about anything she put on. With all this being taken into consideration Kenya still couldn't allow this happen. *Kahless was clearly a little too buzzed, and besides she was her damn coworker for goodness sakes.*

Kahless pulled the straps down to Kenya's tank top and bra, interrupting her panicked thoughts. She started to suck on her breast. Kenya reached out and grabbed a hold of Kahless's hair, as an attempt to stop her. But that seemed to only turn Kahless on even more, surprisingly it turned Kenya on as well. Kahless's red lipstick was now smudged all over Kenya's breast. She pulled Kahless closer.

They both stared at each other breathing heavy. Kenya gripped the back of her neck, and pulled her lips to hers, kissing her roughly. Kenya used her teeth to bite down on Kahless's bottom lip. Kahless undid Kenya's pants, as they continued to kiss and pull each other's hair. *This wasn't right, but it felt so good, a little too good. Why stop?* It's like they both were in this wild mania state, and neither of them wanted to stop despite what their minds were screaming out.

Kenya laid there on the couch in her bra and panties, helping Kahless get out of hers. Within moments they were back on top of each other. Kahless slid Kenya's panties to the side, and then she slid one of her fingers

30

into Kenya's vagina. Kahless slid one finger in at first, then two. Kenya reached up and unhooked Kahless's bra letting her breast free. Kenya took one of her size D cups into her mouth, and sucked around her nipples. She bit down on them with just the right amount of pressure.

Kahless moaned loudly, while biting down on her bottom lip. Her fingers were now moistened from the juices that dripped from the insides of Kenya's pink kitty cat. Kahless reached down and brought her fingers up to her mouth. She slowly sucked Kenya's juices from them, savoring the taste. Kahless then bent down, and sucked on Kenya's bottom lip. Their foreheads, and noses pressed up against each other's. "We should chill right?" Kahless asked panting.

"Yeah we should. My boyfriend comes home soon." Kenya said, Painting as well. But before she knew it they were engaged in another passionate kiss. Kenya didn't know what to do next, but they had already came this far they might as well get each other off. They got into the sixty-nine position. Kenya was on top of Kahless staring right at her vagina, and Kahless laid below staring at Kenya's vagina.

Once again Kenya was clueless. She didn't know what she should do first, so she just followed Kahless's lead. Whatever Kahless did to her she mirrored it. Kenya kissed Kahless's clean-shaven pussy lips, and then she sucked them, parting both lips with her tongue. Kenya ran her tongue back and forth between Kahless's clitoris, and her vaginal opening. She gently bit down on her slightly erect clitoris. Kenya was sure this was sending the same chilled feeling through Kahless's body, as it was hers.

Kahless was slightly shaking, and getting wetter and

31

wetter as they continued. This was Kenya's proof and motivation to continue. Kenya took her finger, and dipped it in and out of Kahless's pussy. She raised her fingers towards her mouth. Kenya closed her eyes tightly before sucking them. She was immediately relieved. *She liked it. She actually liked the way it tasted. Never in a million years did she ever think she'd be in this position, doing this and actually enjoying it.*

Her nipples were so hard that her nipple rings kept moving back and forth through them. Kenya leaned back down, and stuck her tongue in between Kahless's pussy as far as she could. Kenya stroked her wet pussy with her tongue, using the same exact care Kahless was taking with her kitty cat. Kenya moved her tongue around the insides of Kahless's walls, letting it hit up against them gently.

She played with her clitoris as she did this, causing more of Kahless's juices to come down. Kahless moved her pussy to the rhythm of Kenya's tongue, while Kenya did the same, grinding her pussy on Kahless's lips, and tongue. They dipped their tongues in and out faster, sucking just a little harder. Both of them were moaning loudly. There was no way they could keep the moans from escaping their lips even if they tried.

Kenya gripped her arms around Kahless's thick thighs for support, as she continued to work her tongue. Kahless's legs began to shake. *Or were they shaking?* Kenya couldn't tell, because her own body was having a mini earthquake of it's own. Kenya could feel her juices squirting out at the same time Kahless's began rushing out. Kenya never came so hard in her life. She wanted to lie there, and bask in her orgasm, but she had to hurry and get cleaned up.

She picked her head up from in between Kahless's thighs. Kenya's heart nearly jumped out of her chest at what she saw before her. There stood her boyfriend by the front door with his pants to his ankles. His dick in his hand, jerking himself to an orgasm of his own.

CHAPTER FOUR

Case of The Ex

Teff was positioned in the middle of his bed. His sweat pants and boxers were pulled mid way down his thighs. He held his hard penis in his hand, stroking it as he watched Monica slowly get undressed for him. Teff watched her closely as she wiggled out of her panties, and unhooked her bra. "I hope you like what you see?" She reached down and stuck two fingers in between her thighs, and then brought them to her lips. She sucked them in such a seductive manner.

It was completely understandable why Teff was staring so hard. Teff licked his lips and nodded his head in approval. "Girl bring your fine self here now!" He said, indicating to her with his index finger. Monica walked slowly over to the bed in which he laid, and slowly crawled on top of it. She positioned herself in between his legs, palming as much of her breast in her hands as she could. Monica then angled her head slightly, and brought one of her breast up to her mouth, sucking on it gently.

She made circles around her nipples while still looking

Teff square in the eyes. She stopped herself, and slowly made her way closer to his hard penis, which stood at full attention. She caressed it with her hands, and then she kissed the head of it. Monica stuck her tongue out and licked around the head of his penis, then up and down the shaft of it. Teff looked down at her, as she looked up at him.

Teff's dick was disappearing then reappearing between her sexy full lips. "Spit on it for me. Make it nice and wet!" Teff whispered to her. Monica did just that. She deep throated his penis, letting her saliva wet every inch of his penis. She then pulled it from her lips, spitting on the head of it. Monica shoved it back down her throat again, sucking it wildly, and smacking her lips. "This dick tastes so good daddy." She moaned with her mouth full.

Teff began to feel that all too familiar feeling in his nut sack. He jerked back abruptly, as an attempt to stop Monica, before she caused him to explode in the back of her throat. Monica leaned back and smiled knowingly. "How you want me daddy?" She asked, while rubbing her hands on her clitoris in a circular motion. Teff motioned for her to turn around with his finger. "Why don't you ever Dance for me?" He asked.

"Because you never asked me too." She said grinning. "Ok well now I'm telling you. Turn around!" Monica did as she was told. She stood up and turned around. She began to make her ass cheeks clap together. She held on to the bedpost to help keep her balance. Teff laid there watching her, his penis standing up hard and straight. He was about to make her get on all fours, when his cell phone began to ring.

Monica stopped shaking her ass, and turned her head

to look at him. Teff fiddled with his phone, squinting at the screen to see who the hell was interrupting them. Tamara is what his phone read. "Oh hell no!" He said under his breath as he hit the decline button. "Not tonight!" He turned his phone off, and sat it on the nightstand beside his bed. Teff directed his attention back towards Monica, who was still standing in front of him naked. She had more curves than a racetrack. Her body simply looked amazing.

"Did I tell your ass to stop?" He asked, while grinning. "No!" Monica replied, grinning back at him. She began to make one of her butt cheeks jump up and down. "Who was that though? It's late… Who would be calling you this late at night?" She asked, while still dancing. Before Teff could even lie to her he heard a knock at his front door. *Maybe he was just hallucinating.* He thought.

He listened closely this time. Sure enough someone was banging at his front door. "Fuck!" He cursed aloud. "Want me to go get it? I can tell whoever it is that you're not home. That is if you want me too…" Monica began climbing down from where she stood on the bed. Teff jumped up at once, pulling his pants and boxers up over his stiff penis. "No! No! No! I'll get it!" He yelled. "You stay right here! Until I get back babe. Please don't move!"

Monica shot him a funny look. "Are you sure? I can get it for you… you know… It's not a big deal Teff." "No that's ok! I'm sure! I'll be right back! just give me five minutes! Just five minutes! Please don't move!" Teff said in a hurried tone. He walked out of his bedroom, closing the door tightly behind him. He already knew that this had to be Tamara. His thoughts were bouncing all over the place.

Why did she have to come tonight? out of all nights she decided tonight. Tamara was his ex girlfriend. They have been separated for sometime now, but they've decided to remain friends. She was able to see whom she wanted, and he saw whoever he wanted in return. Occasionally they would engage in sexual intercourse together. I mean how could he not. Thick girls were his weakness and Tamara was the epitome of that. Tamara was from Atlanta, so she was thick as shit no need to go into great detail. She had a very cute face and a nice little southern accent, when she spoke. Tamara was okay for the most part. However she just had a lot of issues with her. If it wasn't one thing it was another, and he couldn't deal with that. But besides the sex he really did care about her, so he didn't mind her coming by from time to time. Tonight just wasn't the night though.

Teff cut his thoughts short, and pulled his sweatpants down a bit to make them seem baggy, as a way to hide his mid erection. Since he was shirtless he had nothing to hide it with. "I'm coming! Damn stop banging!" Teff had no idea what he was going to tell Tamara, as he approached the door his thoughts were still running wild. He looked through the peephole. There stood Tamara with her arms folded in front of her.

Her face was all screwed up into a frown. Teff decided right then and there, that he wasn't even going to let her ass in. He had been trying to get with Monica's fine ass for months. Now that he had her where he wanted her. He wasn't about to let anything jeopardize that. Teff took a deep breath, and cleared his throat, before opening the door to step out into the hallway. "Tamara I'm busy!"

Before he could get another word out Tamara pushed passed him, and started ranting about things he couldn't make out at the time. "Tamara!" He called after her. "Tamara I'm busy! You have to come back another time!" "But I really could use your company right now Teff." She pouted. "Well can't it wait Tamara? I'm kind of in the middle of something right now." Tamara stood back and looked Teff over.

"Oh I see. You have company… You said you would always be here for me, and now you are kicking me out! Because you have company over!" She began to cry. Teff gripped the sides of his face. He was frustrated, and beginning to get nervous. "Tamara don't cry. I'm here for you, really I'am. I'm just busy right now." She began to cry louder. Teff tried his hardest to hush her up before Monica over heard the commotion. But it was too late.

When he looked up Monica was standing there in his t-shirt. "What's going on Teff? Is everything okay?" She asked with a concerned look on her face. "Yeah Monica everything's okay, just give me a minute will you." Monica rolled her eyes. "Well everything doesn't look ok." Monica reached for a box of tissues that sat on the coffee table. She snatched a few pieces from it. She then walked over to Tamara and sat down beside her.

"Are you okay?" She asked handing her the tissues. Tamara took them from her hands and cried even harder. Monica looked up at Teff who was motioning her to get Tamara out. She fanned him off. Teff couldn't believe Tamara was over here crying and carrying on, and to piss him off further she now had Monica caught up in her web. Teff threw his hands up in the air, and then plopped down on the couch next to Monica.

About 15 minutes later Tamara and Monica were laughing, and talking like old friends. Teff couldn't believe this shit. *He knew Tamara intended to fuck up his night. This was not the first time she has popped up unannounced. But if she thought he was going to ask Monica to leave on account of her she was sadly mistaken. I'm going to have my fun whether she leaves or not.* He thought. Teff stood up directly in front of them, and dropped his sweats and boxers, catching them both completely off guard.

His penis stood at full attention. He had made his move. *Now either one of them had the choice to get up and leave. Teff was hoping that if Tamara did choose to leave, that she did so drama free.* But to his surprise she didn't get angry nor did she get up to leave. Instead she grabbed his waist and pulled him closer to her. She took his hard penis into her mouth. Tamara continued to inch his penis into her mouth until it was no longer visible.

Teff put his head back. It's been awhile since Tamara and him last hooked up. Its funny how soon he forgot how good Tamara performed oral sex. Tamara had his full attention. He'd almost forgotten Monica was still in the room. Until he felt her breath, and wet lips on his neck and shoulders. Monica kissed and sucked his neck, working her way up to his ear lobes. Teff took one of his hands, and pulled Tamara's hair out of her face.

With his free hand he reached around, and gripped one of Monica's ass cheeks. "Mmmm," She moaned in his ear. Monica leaned in and kissed him roughly, biting down on his bottom lip. Tamara continued to suck and wet his penis. Monica stopped kissing Teff, and walked back over to the couch. She began to help Tamara get completely undressed. Once Tamara was nude Monica took the t-shirt of Teff's off and tossed it.

She got on her knees next to Tamara, and began licking Teff's balls. "Awwww shit!" Teff moaned. Monica began to kiss Tamara until she loosed her grip on Teff's dick. Monica then took him into her mouth and sucked the head of his penis, making a popping sound each time she pulled it from her lips. Tamara then made her way back to his penis, kissing Monica in the process.

They went back and forth until Teff stopped them both. "How do you want me daddy?" Monica said in that seductive tone of hers. Giving Teff the urge to bend her over right then and there, but he kept his cool. "I want the both of you to lie back on the couch, and spread your legs for me. Both of them did as they were told. Tamara put one of her legs behind her head to show off. Teff moved his coffee table out of the way, and then got down on his knees.

He began to rub Tamara's clitoris, as he pushed her legs further apart. Teff ran his tongue up and down her wet pink vagina, stopping shortly to suck on her clitoris. He moved back and forth between the two of them, pleasing them both at the same time. "More tongue baby," Tamara moaned out, while grabbing on to his ears, and grinding her waist and vagina harder on his face. Teff stuck his tongue deeper, causing her to climax.

He stood up satisfied. He then moved over to get Monica to her happy ending as well. Once he was done he stood back, and stepped out of his clothes completely. "Come on to the bedroom." He said, smacking both of their asses, as they walked towards the bedroom. Once in the room Monica and Tamara quickly got on the bed. They wasted no time kissing one another, moving their tongues in and out of each others mouth, biting and sucking each others nipples.

Teff was shocked as hell. He really didn't expect Tamara to be cool with any of this, but on the other hand. He damn sure wasn't going to stop them. He stood back and watched the both of them go at it for a few more moments. They were both all over each other. Teff couldn't believe they way they were kissing, and grabbing each other's ass. Teff's dick got harder just from the site. He stroked it, as he climbed up on the bed, and got in between them.

He grabbed a handful of breast on one side and a handful of ass on the other. He couldn't decide whom to fuck first. Both females seemed to be attractive to each other, so he decided to go with Monica. Since he had already fucked Tamara plenty of times. Teff sat up a bit, grabbing Monica's waist and pulling her back onto his dick, her warmth and juices drenching it right away.

Tamara slid up on to one of the pillows and spread her legs. Monica took her two fingers and dipped them inside of Tamara's pussy, and then pulled them out and licked them. She then spread Tamara's pussy lips with her two fingers and began licking it, moaning loudly each time she felt Teff's dick deep inside her stomach. She gripped the sheets between her fingers as tightly as she could.

"Oh my gosh Teff!" She screamed, as he slammed into her from behind. Monica's ass cheeks clapped its on beat against his mid section. Teff pulled out and smacked her ass roughly and then moved her out of the way. He grabbed Tamara by her ankles, pulling her from the head of the bed. "Let's go babe up top. You know how I like it" Teff positioned himself in the spot he'd just pulled her from.

Tamara straddled him, taking all of his 10 inches inside of her. She immediately did a spin putting herself in the reverse cowgirl position. She reached down and gripped his ankles to support herself, as she bounced her ass up and down on his hard dick. Meanwhile Monica climbed her way to the top of the bed and sat on his face. She gripped both her hands tightly on the headboard, slapping her hands against it, as she road his face.

Teff dug his hands into her butt cheeks, burying his face deeper, fucking her with his tongue. Both ladies began to moan and scream aloud. Both of them were caught up in the middle of their third climax. "Teff... Teff I love this dick!" He could hear Tamara moaning out, as her juices leaked out, wetting his pubic hairs. Tamara felt Teff about to reach a climax of his own, so she got off him and moved her behind back on to his chest some.

She swiftly put his dick into her mouth once more. Monica came around front, and began to suck his balls. Teff put both his hands over his face. He couldn't even begin to describe how powerful and in charge he felt at that very moment. Pure Blissful pleasure is what seeped through his veins. Tamara moaned, and sucked until she felt Teff's body jerk, and his cum explode out filling the back of her throat. She sucked until every drop was released.

CHAPTER FIVE

Sour Apples On Fifth

"All that giggling you doing you're going to get our Asses caught!" Mecca whispered into Demi's ear, while he kissed and sucked on her neck. "I'm trying not too! But you know that's my spot you're kissing." Demi said, while gripping the back of Mecca's neck. She gently tugged on his beard pulling his lips towards hers. Demi stuck her tongue in his mouth and intertwined it with his, sucking on his bottom lip at the same time.

"You're so fucking sexy." She said, pulling away from their lip lock. "Come on let's go back on the selling floor, before someone catches us!" Demi grabbed Mecca's arm and pulled him towards the stock room door. Mecca tugged in the opposite direction, pulling her back towards him. "What if I want us to get caught? Huh? Huh?" He said in between kisses. He slowly lured Demi right back in. Demi giggled some more, as she put a little distance In between them with her hand.

"Now you know better! We can't do this!" "And why can't we? Who says we can't?" Mecca said, trying to move her hand out the way. "Our damn boss silly. We get caught and that's both of our Asses. We would be in a heap of trouble! And I can't afford to lose my job Mecca!" Demi snapped at him. "Don't worry about that. I know someone that's over our boss." Said Mecca. "Who?" Demi asked in disbelief.

"Him!" Mecca said, letting his jeans, and briefs hit the floor. His hard dick curved over his thigh. Before Demi could object, he reached out and pulled her hand towards it, giving her no choice but to caress it. "Come on five minutes. We been in here this long we might as well." Mecca stared at Demi with a pleading look in his eyes. Demi looked at his dick, then back towards the stockroom door.

"Just five minutes. I promise it will be worth it. You know you want too." He whispered, while kissing her neck again, making it extremely hard for her to say no. "Okay! Five minutes!" Demi said, in a hurried tone. She quickly made a mad dash over to the stockroom door. Demi dragged some boxes with laptops, and other products in front of it. She then turned, and kicked off one of her converse sneakers.

She swiftly pulled one of her legs out of her denim jeans. Demi walked towards Mecca. They met each other in the middle of the floor with another rough wet lip lock. Their hands roamed each other's body, caressing and squeezing each other's private areas. "This better be fucking worth it!" Demi whispered in his ear, while she rubbed his bald-head and inhaled his sent. Mecca turned her around, and pulled her panties down.

He reached under her bra, and cuffed both of her breasts. He squeezed her hard nipples between his thumbs and index fingers. Demi bit down on her bottom lip. "Hurry up! Would you put it in already! Hurry before you get us caught!" Demi said looking back at him impatiently. "Shut up!" Mecca said, smacking her ass, and then grabbing the back of her neck. In one swift motion he entered her.

Demi gasped as she took all of him in. Mecca moved in and out of her slowly at first, then picked up his speed a little bit. He slowed his pace once more. Demi's vagina walls had a tight grip around his penis, so tight, he was afraid he might cum already. Mecca wanted it to be worth her wild. They had only just gotten started he couldn't give in now. He began to slow his pace down to a slow hump.

Mecca had so much adrenalin pumping through his body from the thrill of having sex while on the clock. They could be caught at any given moment. It was all so exciting and almost too good to be true. Hell Demi's pussy was almost too good to be true. Her vagina walls gripped around his dick tighter. Mecca could feel his knees starting to buckle beneath him. He gripped the back of her neck tighter and dug his other hand into the left side of her waist.

"What the fuck are you doing back there? Why are you going so slow?" Demi struggled to turn her head around and look back at him. " Fuck me harder!" She snarled at him in the most aggressive manner, but still managed to look so completely irresistible and sexy. "Shut up!" Mecca whispered back to her, forcing her to turn back around. He spread his feet further apart for added support.

He put his head back. All he could hear was the wet sticky sounds Demi's pussy made each time he stroked it, and a light thumping sound each time Demi's hands tapped against the boxes in front of her. Mecca stopped moving, and let Demi back into him. He quickly looked over his shoulder to make sure they were still alone. Once he saw they were still in the clear, Mecca put his head back once more and closed his eyes. Before he could get the chance to zone out again he felt Demi knock his arm away from her neck.

She eased his dick away from her wetness, and turned to face him. She looked frustrated. "Get down on the floor!" She demanded. "What? Girl you're crazy! It's cold down there!" said Mecca hesitant. "Get your fucking ass on the floor now!" Demi said repeating herself. Only this time she pushed him as she said it. Mecca quickly laid down on the floor.

His dick stood straight up, all of Demi's wetness still covering it. Demi quickly took off her other converse, and slipped her jeans completely off. She eased herself down onto his stiff dick. She gripped a hold of the white-framed name badge that rested around his neck. She removed hers, so not to hit him in the face as she rode him. Demi stood up on her feet, and began to bounce up and down on his dick.

She gripped the badge tight with one hand. She ran her fingers through his soft beard with her free hand. "Damn girl could you slow down! You're going to make me…" Mecca's voice trailed off. He couldn't even finish the rest of his statement. Because Demi kept clenching, and releasing the head of his penis, tighter between her vagina's walls and it's lips. Demi stared down at him as she continued to bounce up, and down.

She knew she was putting it on him, and she took

pleasure in watching him try to hold out. She slowed her pace down to a very slow grind. Demi slid her pussy all the way up to the head of his dick, tightened her vagina walls around it, and then slid down slowly. Mecca ran his hands over his head, and then covered his face. "Shit girl! What are you trying to do to me? Fuck! Awe shit!" He continued to curse and make noise.

Demi put her finger to her lips, indicating to him that he was making to much noise, but he couldn't see her. Demi reached down and slipped her panties off, which dangled from her ankle. She balled them up, and stuffed them into Mecca's mouth. " You better not fucking cum yet! You said this would be worth it!" Demi reversed on top of him. She was giving Mecca a full view of her round ass, and his dick appearing, and then disappearing deep inside of her. She bounced up and down on him, while she played with her clitoris.

As she began to reach her climax she felt Mecca's dick began to pulsate inside of her. She knew He was about to reach his climax. She bounced up and down, faster and harder. Demi slid off his dick just in time. Mecca's semen shot out and squirted all over her stomach. Mecca stayed positioned on the floor, while Demi on the other hand quickly ran to a corner to clean herself up.

She slipped her things back on. She was fully dressed by the time Mecca decided to get up and get himself together. He sat on the floor pulling his jeans up. Demi walked over to him and kneeled down in front of him. She was so close to him that their foreheads kissed. Their skin was still clammy. Demi looked him directly in the eyes. "You better not tell a soul. Not one single soul." She licked her lips, and then turned to leave, leaving Mecca scrambling on the floor to get himself together.

CHAPTER SIX

Vices

One could only exercise but for so much. How much exercise does it take to clear a clouded mind? Tanner hadn't yet to figure this out. He had been running on the treadmill for well over an hour now, and still he couldn't decimate the silent war that was taking place inside of his head. Tanner's thoughts were eating him up on the inside. It was becoming more difficult, to keep them from tearing through, the last few pieces of sanity that he held on too.

This was the only something he had, helping to keep the thoughts that haunted him, from making an appearance on the outside. Tanner smashed the red stop button on the treadmill, causing it to come to a slow stop. He leaned over the treadmill, his chest rising and falling heavily. He wiped some sweat from his forehead, right before it connected with his pupils. Tanner removed his headphones and looked around.

The gym was completely empty, besides the staff, a ridiculously buff dude lifting weights in a far corner, and a woman had just walked towards the ladies locker room.

Tanner stared at her momentarily. *She looked like... Like.* "Never mind!" He said out loud, while shaking his head. *My mind must be playing tricks on Me.* He thought to himself. Tanner looked down at his watch. It was 2am. What else was there for him to do now?

He had taken advantage of just about everything the gym had to offer. He had done boxing, weights, push ups, pull ups, crunches. Tanner even rode the bike for a while. He didn't want to go home. He wasn't ready too. Tanner was still too pumped up, and if he went home now, he knew for sure his anger would have him do something his character normally wouldn't do. "No way. I can't go home." He said to himself.

Maybe a walk along the FDR would do him some good. He thought. It sounded like a plan to him. Tanner grabbed his towel, and threw it over his head to absorb his sweat. He walked towards the men's changing room, but suddenly stopped short in his tracks. He heard what sounded like music coming from a dimly lit corridor. His mind told him to mind his own business, but curiosity had him by the neck.

He made a left towards the direction of the music. Tanner walked through two double doors. He was immediately overwhelmed with a burst of steam, and the smell of Chlorine. The corridor split into two directions. One direction lead to a swimming pool, and the other was leading to a sauna. Tanner was slightly shocked. He had been a member of this gym for almost two years now, and he never knew either of the two existed.

Tanner removed the towel from his head, so he could listen closer. What sounded like music moments ago was now clear as a bell. It wasn't music being played from a radio, but a woman singing. The signing was coming from the direction of the Sauna, so he slowly walked in that direction. The closer he got to the sauna, the more his vision became a bit of a blur from the thick steam. However he could still hear the woman's voice loud and clear.

Tanner couldn't make out the song she was belting out. Nevertheless she sounded so melodic. Her voice was beautiful. Tanner inched his way closer to the sauna room door and peeped in. There she sat naked with a thick white towel wrapped around her body, and one wrapped around her head. One Headphone was in her ear, and the other one was hanging out. Her eyes were closed shut, and her legs were up on the bench. Her knees were almost touching her chest, her arms were wrapped around them.

Tanner waved his hand in front of his face to try to eliminate some of the steam. His eyes widen. He couldn't believe his luck. *It's her*. He thought. She was beautiful. Even with her hair tied up in a towel. She seemed at such peace. Tanner didn't want to interrupt her, or let her know he had seen her. Tanner turned to leave, but the slippery floor beneath him caused him to lose his balance. Before he could grab a hold to something he went crashing to the marble floor.

The woman immediately jumped, and ran towards the other exit. But stopped in her tracks when she heard Tanner yell out in agony. Tanner had used his hand to break his fall, and ended up spraining his wrist. "Are you ok?" She called out to him from where she stood. "I'm fine." Tanner mumbled, as he tried to use his other hand to get up. Each time he attempted to pull himself up, his sneakers went sliding, and he fell back down.

The woman stood there watching him struggle for a few moments. Once she saw that he wasn't trying to harm her, or anything of that nature. She quickly ran over to help him up, and get him over to the bench. Tanner leaned his body against her little frame, as they slowly walked over to the bench and sat down. "Are you okay?" She asked again as she examined his wrist that was already beginning to swell. "Yea I'll be okay." Tanner said with his head down. He was slightly embarrassed from his fall, and her now knowing he was peeping in on her.

"It's sprained." She said firmly. Tanner laughed "Oh yeah, and how would you know? Are you some kind of doctor or something?" "No, but I'm a physical therapist, and I think I know a sprained wrist when I see one!" Tanner felt a bit silly after she said that. "Oh… I'm sorry. Please forgive my sarcasm… I'm sorry." Tanner apologized. "Don't be." She said, while revealing a smile that lit up the whole room.

She continued speaking. "You didn't know. I have just one question for you though. What were you doing back here with these sneakers on? You could have broken your neck!" Tanner scratched his head, while looking around for something that he could use as an excuse to answer her question. But came up with nothing. He let out a deep sigh. "Honestly I had no business back here. I was actually on my way to get changed, when I heard your beautiful voice. I was well… I was… I was just being nosy." Tanner said with his head lowered a bit.

She smiled "well you see where nosy got your butt." Both of them exploded with laughter. "Yea you're right! Go ahead and laugh at my pain." Tanner said. She looked at him. For a brief moment their eyes were fixed on each other's, unable to break free. Tanner couldn't help but notice how happy she actually looked. It was hard not to notice how full of life her eyes were.

She must still not know. He wondered what she saw in his eyes. Hopefully not the pain, and hurt, that he was actually feeling deep down inside. "Come on, let me help you out of here." She said interrupting his thoughts. She grabbed his other hand, and they slowly walked towards the door, and down the corridor. Half way down she turned to him. " Well I have to go back, and get my things out of the locker. Do you think you'll be alright from here?" He laughed, "Yeah I'll be just fine, it's just a sprained wrist."

She laughed, and then began to turn around. "Well it was nice meeting you." She smiled and waved. She then headed back through the double doors. Tanner stood there and listened, until the sound of her footsteps faded to nothing, just an awkward silence.Tanner made his way to the locker room and grabbed his gym bag. He pulled his old college hoodie over his head, grabbed his hat, scarf, gloves, and slipped them on. Lastly he threw his towel in his bag, and then headed towards the exit.

The cold winter air kissed his wet salty skin, immediately sending a chill through his body. *So much for walking along the FDR,* He thought. "Damn I should have worn a jacket." Tanner said aloud. He was Mad at himself, because now he had no choice but to go home. Tanner pulled his hoodie over his head tighter, as he headed further downtown. He stopped at a nearby deli, and grabbed a cup of coffee, along with some aspirin.

He was hoping it would kill off the pain he felt from his wrist. Tanner couldn't help but think about the woman he had stumbled in on back at the gym. She was beautiful up close. The joy that was in her eyes, and her smile stayed with him. Tanner wondered *what she was so happy from, or who even. If only she knew what he had done, then maybe she wouldn't be so happy. Maybe she would feel the same pain as he did.*

Tanner took a sip from his coffee, and shook his head. *Damn I didn't even get her name, just to make sure…* He cut his own thought short with another thought. *Maybe I should go back.* He started thinking. *I should have waited to see if she needed someone to walk her safely home.* "Damn! It is late!" He said under his breath, but as soon as he looked up he was approaching his building. Tanner could feel his temper rising the closer he got to his lobby entrance.

He slowly pushed through the lobby doors. The doorman looked up from his article and greeted him with a "good night sir." Tanner smiled halfheartedly, then headed towards the elevator. He pushed the button for the 27th floor. He patiently waited for the doors to open. Once he exited the elevator he began to walk slower, almost to the point where he was dragging himself. Tanner slowly opened his door, and entered his apartment.

It was the exact way he had left it for the past two weeks. Old records were scattered all over his living room floor. His grandmother's record player lay amongst them. A bottle of Hennessy still sat unopened next to a half eaten box of cereal. A blanket and some pillows covered his sectional. He hadn't slept in his room in weeks. Tanner shook his head at the mess. He turned and walked into his kitchen.

Tanner was about to open the fridge, when his eyes caught a glimpse of a magnetic picture frame. It held a picture of his now ex girlfriend. He immediately became enraged, smacking the magnet, sending it crashing to the floor. It cracked into several pieces. Tanner reached down and grabbed the photo. He tore it into little pieces. He then grabbed the bottle of Hennessy and held it tight in his hands. Tanner still couldn't bring himself to open it.

He hadn't taken a drink since the day his best friend died in a car accident, while intoxicated. Even with all the pain his heart felt at that very moment he still couldn't bring himself to do it. He turned to the sink and began to pour the liquor out. Once it was empty, he slammed it down. This sent a pain through his left wrist, bringing him back to reality. Tanner went into the bathroom and ran some cold water over his face, then popped two aspirin. Tanner stood there staring at himself in the mirror.

He looked like Thursday and it was only Monday. He was in desperate need of a shave and hair cut. You could barely tell his eyes were hazel, they were so red, and filled with rage. He ran his hand through his thick curly hair. "Man that woman back at the gym must of thought I was a crazy person." He mumbled, while smiling at the thought of running into Her. His mood softened a bit. He had to see her again, but this time he wouldn't look like a maniac.

Tanner walked back into the living room and began to clean up. As he cleaned he threw away all that was left behind by his ex. The more he cleaned, and threw away all her things, the better he felt. Before he knew it his place was spick and span. Tanner went into his bedroom and plopped down on his king size bed. He was exhausted. He laid there in deep thought fighting his sleep, until he could no longer hold out...

January had just arrived in front of her building. She

slowed her bike to a complete stop, and walked it over to the side of her building, where she locked it up. She ran up the steps to her brownstone and quickly opened the door. January stepped in. She immediately turned on the lights to the lower part of her place. January took her gym sneakers off and placed them on a rug by the door. She hung the rest of her things on the nearby coat rack, which was empty, so she knew no one else was home.

Therefore she didn't even waste her time checking the rest of the apartment. This was nothing new to her. January grabbed her gym bag, and tossed it downstairs in the basement. She was in no mood to wash clothes. In fact her body was very tense. She had been up since six in the morning, and here it was now 3am, going on 4am. She walked into her kitchen, and grabbed a bottle of red wine, along with a wine glass.

January hit the lights once more, and then headed upstairs. She sat on her bed and poured herself a glass of wine. She took a sip, immediately it entered her bloodstream making her a bit more relaxed. "I need a damn shower!" She said fanning herself. She was still feeling sweaty from her workout earlier and the sauna room. January made her way to the bathroom. She flipped on the lights, which ran across the long bathroom mirror.

Then she began to take her clothes off. January stood in front of the mirror in the nude, looking at her body, which was in perfect shape. She had nice lean arms, a nice four pack, thick thighs, and a nice round ass. She turned her body to the side. January stared at her butt with a childish grin on her face. She then gripped her breast, which sat just right. Her nipples began to harden from her own touch.

January poured herself another glass, as she massaged her neck. She still felt tense. She knew then that she would need a bath instead of a shower. January walked over to the bathroom door, and grabbed her silk robe, quickly slipping it on. She sat at the edge of her bathtub pouring honey, and vanilla scented bubble bath inside. Patiently waiting for the tub to fill. January reached inside her robe, and gripped one of her breast once more.

Her nipples were so hard. She plucked one of them. This sent goose bumps up her thighs. She then squeezed her nipples in between her thumb and index fingers, while closing her eyes, and biting down on her bottom lip. January could feel her clitoris beginning to throb. She crossed her legs tight, as if that would soothe the throbbing. January opened her eyes to see that the tub was almost about to overflow with bubbles.

She immediately turned the gold knobs to shut the water off. She stood up, and let her robe hit the floor, then slowly stepped into the hot water. The smell of the bubble bath, and the hot water was definitely soothing to her entire body. January massaged her neck, and rolled her head in a circular motion. "Why the hell am I so damn tense?" She asked herself, as she reached for the bottle of wine, and bringing it up to her lips.

That's when she suddenly remembered the weird guy who almost killed himself in the Sauna room. She started to chuckle. Now that she was home the whole incident was kind of funny. She wondered *what his story was. His eyes were gorgeous, hypnotizing almost, but they looked so sad. Now that she was thinking about it, he looked rather distraught, but he was definitely handsome, and definitely her type.*

January didn't even notice that she was squeezing her nipples again, but she was. She imagined them being kissed, sucked, and gently bitten down on. The more she thought about this stranger, the more she imagined what she would do to him, or let him do to her rather. January rubbed two of her fingers in a circular motion, massaging her clitoris, which was still throbbing. It was practically begging to be kissed, sucked, and nibbled on. January inserted one of her fingers into her vagina.

She slowly moved it in and out, and then she inserted another finger. January moved them both in and out of her vagina walls, pushing them as far as she could. Even though her fingers felt good they weren't quite getting the job done. She needed some type of penetration. Her fingers were just teasing her. January climbed out of the tub. She ran butt naked over to a little cabinet, underneath the bathroom sink, and opened it.

She pulled out a black rectangular box. Inside was a gold vibrator. January removed it, then quickly ran back over to the tub, and stepped back in. She laid her head back, and started to imagine how the stranger looked underneath his clothing. She wondered if he had a large or a small penis, or something In between. It didn't take long for her mind to get carried away. January was in deep thought. She put one of her legs up on the tub ledge, and slowly inserted the vibrated.

"Ahhhh yes!" She moaned, as quietly as she could. January twisted the device, and it began to vibrate. She moved it in and out of her vagina opening. January envisioned herself gripping the back of the strangers head with one hand, while her nails dug into his back with the other, him swiftly stroking his penis in out of her wetness.

She continued to moan silently, as she gripped the vibrator tighter.

January put her other leg up, and quickly twisted the device again. It changed from a fast vibration to a slow pulse. She moved her hand faster and bit down on her bottom lip. She could feel herself about to climax." Mmmmm, Ooh, mmmmm" She whimpered through her clenched lips. January put her head back as she released herself, letting out a deep breath. Her eyes remained closed, but in her mind they still looked into the strangers.

She wanted to hold on to what she envisioned, but after a few moments the vibrator began to become annoying. January slowly opened her eyes to remove and place it to the side. She was completely shocked to see Sean standing by the door watching her. It frightened her so much, that she jumped back, and ended up hitting her head. "Honey I didn't know you were home!" She said nervously and bashfully, not sure how much he had witnessed, if anything at all.

"I just got in. I'm exhausted." He said, letting out a sigh. Sean looked like something was bothering him. "Care to join me? I'll give you a nice massage!" January said slipping the vibrator behind her head. Sean began to fidget. "Not tonight Hun I'm beat!" His eyes shifted back and forth, then they fell to the floor. He stared at the floor a few moments before speaking again. "Can you please wrap things up though? I need to shower before I come to bed." Sean said flatly, before turning to leave.

January frowned, as she released the drain letting the water flow out. She stood up and turned on the shower. She was the least bit bother by Sean's attitude. Well at least not tonight. His suspicious actions the past few months have sort of become the norm. January grabbed some body wash, and began to lather up her washcloth. She could still feel her clitoris throbbing between her legs. She squeezed her legs closed as tight as she could. She wanted more. "Damn! All this from some stranger. I don't even know his darn name!" She said to herself, as she continued to wash. January had to see him again. Even though she shouldn't be thinking this, she secretly hoped too see him again...

"Thanks again Denis man for hooking me up as always! I know it's late and you were probably in for the night." Tanner was speaking to his barber, while he stared at his freshly trimmed beard and haircut. "No big deal Tee! You know you've been my homie since way back. We are like brothers man." Said Denis. Tanner turned to him and embraced him, while placing a fifty-dollar bill in his hand at the same time. "Man I already told you your money is no good here." Said Denis.

Tanner grinned, "Well pretend someone dropped it! See you in two weeks." He quickly threw his gym bag over his shoulder, and left the shop, before Denis could object. The gates to the shop were down. The barbershop had been closed for several hours now, but Tanner had called Denis, and asked for a favor, and like always he delivered. Tanner walked quickly in the direction of his gym. He had been going there everyday after work in hopes that he would run into the woman he'd met a few days ago, but he hadn't seen her.

He figured it was due to him going early, so tonight he decided to go in late, really late. He decided to go around the same time as that first night in the sauna. Tanner walked along the FDR drive in deep thought. He couldn't believe he was acting like this over a woman he didn't even know. He couldn't believe he was going crazy over a woman that wasn't even his own, but then again just weeks ago he also couldn't believe he thought he had a woman all his own.

Unknown to him she had been sleeping with a coworker of hers. Tanner felt a pain in the bottom of his stomach. To think he was about to make the biggest mistake of his life, by proposing to his now ex girlfriend. Tanner shook his head still in disbelief. He had actually gone out, and hand picked a ring for his ex. He wanted to make sure it was perfect, so he asked her best friend to help him decide. Tanner went all out too; just to find out she was unfaithful.

At first he was in complete shock and total disbelief, so he followed her, and her lover's every move for two weeks. Once he had seen with his own eyes she was cheating on him. He called everything off. As a result Tanner went into this slump of depression for months, but now here he was with this chilling feeling all over his body, dying to see this stranger woman again. Tanner felt another chill sweep over him; causing him to push his hands deeper inside of his coat pockets.

He wasn't sure if this was some sort of sign, or something. "Should he even pursue her?" Tanner whispered to himself. He felt guilty. This felt wrong, but nevertheless he continued on. Once inside the gym he did a quick scan of the entire room. Again it was damn near empty besides the staff, that same buff dude, but now he had a companion with him, and of course himself. Tanner instantly began to feel slightly disappointed.

He headed towards the males locker room. He quickly

took off his outerwear and locked up his things. He grabbed his towel, water, and headphones, and walked towards the exit. Tanner was about to head for the treadmill, when he happened to glance down the dimly lit corridor. That's when he remembered the sauna and the pool. He quickly slapped his own head. "Damn I totally forgot about the damn sauna! I probably would have been seen her by now. If only I remembered it even existed!"

Tanner quickly moved in the direction of the sauna. He walked through the double doors, as he got closer to the sauna room he began to take off his sneakers, and clothing. He wasn't going to make a fool of him self again. Tanner sat his things down on the floor where he could keep an eye on them. Tanner wrapped his towel tightly around his waist, before taking a deep breath, and then entering the room. The room was full of steam.

Tanner fanned his hand in front of his face to kind of clear his view. The room was empty. There was no sign of her. Tanner sucked his teeth and took a seat on the bench. He sat back, and closed his eyes. He was beginning to feel sorry for himself all over again. He sat there in deep thought, until the smell of sweet pea, or some sort of flower began to fill his nostrils. He opened his eyes and there she was.

A thick white towel was wrapped around her body, and one around her head. She had her headphones in and her back was turned. She was busy pouring a thick liquid into the vents. Tanner could feel that chill again. He could feel himself freezing up. He didn't know if he should say something to let her know he was there, interrupt her, or leave. Tanner was stuck and at a lost for words, before he could even say anything, or move a muscle.

She turned around and noticed him. "Oh my gosh sheeesh! I'm sorry... I didn't know anyone else was in here." She said faintly with her hand over her chest. Tanner cleared his throat. "No don't be sorry it's my fault. I should have said something." She looked down at the small bottle in her hand. "I hope you don't mind the smell. It's aromatherapy. I'm usually alone in here at night so I... I take advantage." She blurted out. "No it's cool. I love it... I mean it smells good... I mean I don't mind. I don't mind at all."

January laughed at his nervousness, then her eyes lit up. "Hey you're the guy from last week. I almost didn't recognize you. Not so much hair this time." Tanner lowered his head a bit. A simper slowly spread over his face. "Yea it's me. The nosy crazy guy that almost broke his neck." They laughed. "Oh how's the wrist?" She said reaching for his hand. "The wrist is doing well. I wrapped it for a few days and put some ice on it. I think I'm going to live."

They both laughed again. "I'm sorry I don't think I got the chance to properly introduce myself. I know you're probably thinking I'm some maniac, but I'm not. My name is Tanner." He said clutching her hand. "And I'm January." She said smiling. "January that's a nice name. Were you born in January?" "No I'm named after my grandmother who passed away." "Oh I'm sorry to hear that. That's a very unfortunate stigma, butt to hell with stigmas!" They both laughed again.

"Yeah it is unfortunate, but like you said to hell with stigmas." January smiled "Mind if I have my hand back though?" She said pointing with her other hand. "Oh of course! Of course you can." Tanner said smiling bashfully.

He didn't even notice that he still held her hand in his. They both took seats on the bench. January shifted in her seat. It was so hard for her not to get lost in his hazel eyes; and it was even harder for her to keep her eyes from wandering over his bare chest. Nevertheless she kept her cool and they continued to chat like old friends.

Tanner had found himself unloading all the drama he had been through with his ex on her. He wanted to stop himself, but once he got going he couldn't stop. He felt as though she should know the truth. He talked so much January barely got a few words in. All she could do was nod and hold her hand over her heart, as if she was being stabbed. By the time they decided to call it a night it was almost 4am.

January yawned, then stood up to stretch. " I'm awfully sorry things went so sour in your relationship. I truly hope some day happiness will be restored back into your heart, so that you can love again. As far as your ex, and the other dude. Just let it go. Anything built over broken glass won't hold up for long. They will get what's coming to them." January looked down as she spoke, so she wouldn't have to look into his eyes. "I think I better get going. It's getting kind of late and I still have to ride home." She mumbled.

"I can walk you if you'd like." Tanner said eagerly. Standing up at the same time. He did not want to end the night just yet. He was in fact enjoying her company. Despite how bad he felt deep down inside. "I don't know. I can't ask you to do that. It is late and besides I rode my bike. I think I could manage" "No really I don't mind." Tanner said reaching out, and touching her hand.

January wasn't sure if it was the steam from the sauna, but her entire body felt like it was on fire from his touch.

She should have declined his offer and removed her hand from his, but instead she slipped her fingers in between his. They stood there staring at each other. January took her free hand, and placed it on the sides of Tanner's face. She rubbed her Hand along the neatly trimmed outline of his facial hairs.

"My gosh you have pretty eyes. I'm sorry to use the word pretty, but that's the only word I can think of right now." She whispered. Tanner smiled. "It's cool I'm use to it. I bet you get that a lot too about your smile." He added. January just blushed, but never looked away from him. She couldn't look away even if she wanted too. Even though he seemed in better spirits since their first encounter, his eyes told a different story.

Shockingly on both of their behalves January reached out, and wrapped her arms around him. She hugged him as tightly as she could. January didn't know what came over her, but it seemed like the right thing to do. Tanner could feel all the pent up anger and hurt he had been holding on to; began to slowly drain from his body. The chilling feeling swept over him again, but he didn't care at this moment if it was a good, or bad sign. Was him being there right or wrong? Tanner just had to have her right there and now.

He pulled her face to his and kissed her passionately. He reached under her towel and palmed her butt cheeks; Tanner squeezed them tight, causing January to stand on her tippy toes. Tanner worked his hands up to her breast and squeezed them both. He took his other hand and attempted to remove her towel, but she grabbed a hold to the ends, before it could fall from her body. "No! Tanner! I can't!" January said, while panting and taking a few steps back.

"Yes you can. You are just afraid, because you barely even know me. Hell you don't know me!" Tanner walked towards her. "You want too though. I know you do. Deep down inside I know you do. Something is telling you too. I have never felt this way about anyone I've just met, so I know you are feeling what I'm feeling too! You're just afraid and that's ok, but I'm telling you. You want this!" He gripped the back of her neck and pulled her lips towards his once more.

"No! Tanner you don't understand! There's something I haven't told you yet!" Tanner gripped her waist, and picked her up in one swift motion. " Whatever it is I don't care. I do not care January!" He kissed her again, as he walked over to the towel shelf, knocking all of the towels down to the damp floor. He sat her down on top of it, and then he lifted one of her legs. He removed his towel from his waist, before getting down on one knee.

"Tanner please wait! You don't understand!" January whispered to him as she slapped his arms, and shoulders, as an attempted to get him to stop. Tanner ignored her. He spread her legs and then buried his face between them. As Tanner licked, sucked and kissed her pussy January's No's turned into soft high-pitched moans. The hits on his shoulders were replaced with lip biting and nail digging.

January wrapped her legs around Tanners shoulders, and griped the back his neck tightly, as she worked her hips. Something inside her mind said this was wrong, and she should stop, but she couldn't. She needed this. Her whole body needed this. She had yarned for a males touch for months. Maybe her mind needed this release as well. Maybe that's why she hugged him, and let him kiss her lips in the first place.

She thought about Sean briefly. Surprisingly she didn't feel as bad as she should have. January kept telling herself that it was his fault that she was even there in the first place. Sean had been the one acting so strange, distant, and sneaky. Sean had also been the one refusing to touch her, as well as refusing to give her a good fuck like she damn well deserved. The more she thought about all the things Sean wasn't doing, or stopped doing, the angrier she became, and the less guilty she felt.

January let out a loud cry that echoed through the halls, as she felt the head of Tanner's hard penis enter her tight wet vagina walls. She was so caught up in her orgasm, that she didn't even notice he had stop pleasuring her pussy, with his mouth and tongue. January started to feel scared and hesitant again. Tanner sensed this, so he switched up and began to stroke her pussy extra slow.

He pressed his arms on the shelf, and leaned over her, his forehead kissing hers. Tanner stared her in her eyes, as he continued to stroke her, bending his knees, and working his hips. He slipped in and out of her wetness. Tanner turned his head and looked away, as he felt her juices began to moisten his pubic hairs. Her juices dripped down to his nut sack. January reached up and pulled his head back to hers.

She gripped his neck firmly once again, while wrapping her legs around his back. Tanner lifted her up and pined her to the wall. They began to go at it, kissing, sucking, and biting each other. January tried to hush her moaning, but she couldn't. The pleasure her entire body was feeling, was too strong to hold in. She held her head back against the wall and let her moans escape. She moaned loudly and dug her nails into Tanner's back, as he slammed hard into her.

Sweat dripped from both of their bodies. Steam and the smell of aromatherapy filled the extremely humid room. Although the steam was nothing compared to the fire that they lit inside of each other. Tanner's strokes quickened fore he was about to reach his climax any minute. January pulled him in close. Her wet lips brushed against his ear. "There is something I didn't get to tell you."

She manages to faintly whisper into his ear. " I'm… I'm… I'm in a relationship" She finally managed to get out at the same time Tanner's warm semen filled her.

Her body quivered as she released herself once more. Tanner could feel his body beginning to get that chilling feeling again, as he looked Directly at January, his eyes filled with Pain. He cleared his throat, and whispered, "I know you are… I already knew…

CHAPTER SEVEN

I Hate That Mushy Shit

"What the fuck do you mean why am I here? I mean what the fuck did you expect me to do Zoey? You fucking changed your number on me and blocked my emails. Every time I go by your job you're not there, or they tell me I just missed you. I know damn well they are only covering for you! Look I just want to talk." David paused briefly. "Baby I miss you... I love you... Please open the door, so we can talk about this on the inside!"

David begged on the other side of Zoey's apartment door, while Zoey stood on the other side of it hanging on to his every word. Her back pressed against it and one hand gripped around the doorknob. A silent war was taking place between her heart and mind. She stood there bouncing all the good against the bad. Zoey had been ducking and dogging David for weeks now. Her mind had nothing more to say to him; however her heart had so many things left unsaid.

It was still angry, it was still hurting, it was still missing him, and lastly it still wanted him. Even after all the wrong he had done to it. Her heart whispered for her to turn the knob and say all that her tongue held prison, but her mind on the other hand was saying, "turn your fucking back. Don't give him a chance to waste your time twice. Don't do it. Don't be silly learn your lesson. Learn this lesson Zoey." She removed her hand from the knob.

"Just leave David! I can't do this anymore. Just forget me... Just let me go, and then I can let you go!" "No I don't want too!" David fired back at her. "Please just give me 10 minutes... Please just 10 minutes... I miss you! I miss you so much! Please just hear me out!" Zoey slammed her fist against the door. "I hate you! I fucking hate you! Why are you doing this? Why keep putting me through this? Just leave David. I can't do this anymore ... Just let me go, so that I can let you go!"

"But what am I doing Zoe? What if I can't let you go? I know you don't hate me. I know you don't! You're just mad! And you have every right to be! I played myself, but most of all I played you! I'm sorry! Please see that I'm sorry! You're not the only one hurting you know... I'm hurting too. Everyday Zoe, but I'm a dude... so I just can't go spilling my feelings in the air to anyone that will listen. I'm here now, and I want to make it right. Babe please just 10 minutes I promise I just want to talk. I just want my friend back Zoe. I made a mistake. I see that now. Please just talk to me. You know I'm not going to stop, so just give me ten…"

Before David could get another word out Zoey turned the doorknob, and swung it open. Her eyes were red and swollen from crying all night. Her hair was pulled up into a messy ponytail. One of David's t-shirts draped over her little physique. Her fists were balled into two tight fists.

Her chest rose and fell fast and heavy. They've had plenty of arguments, and fallouts in the past, but he has never seen her this distraught. Seeing her like this hurt him.

This was all his fault. He had to make it right. He wanted nothing more than to hold her close, and kiss her forehead, tell her how sorry he was. He needed to tell her how much of a stupid asshole he was. David reached out and grabbed her waist. Zoey swung her little fist at him. "Don't fucking touch me David! Say what you have to say! Then fucking leave!" Zoey wiped a tear from the corner of her eye that was trying to escape.

"Look baby I don't want to fight anymore. I don't want you to be mad at me anymore. Please I made a mistake. I never wanted to hurt you. Please know that I'm sorry!" David reached for her again. Zoey swung her fist at him; Her punches missing his face by a long shot. Being that she was much shorter than him. Zoey's fist ended up landing between his chest and midsection.

"You're not fucking sorry David! You're not fucking sorry! I hate you! How could you be so selfish and hurt me? I'm the only one that's there for you. Every time you needed me I was there! No one else! And you treat me like shit. The only person that loves you more than you love yourself! You play me! Me! The only person that pushes you to do better." Her tears fell freely down her face as she hit, and screamed at him.

"You're an egotistic! Selfish! Bastard! All you do is think about yourself and what you want!" David didn't want to mess things up further by voicing his opinion, or objecting to anything that she said, so he let her take out her frustration on him for a few moments more. David then reached down and grabbed her wrists with one hand. He

71

then swept her up into his arms in one swift motion. " Yes I fucked up! I fucked up okay!" He raised his voice so that he could get her to listen. Then he quickly lowered it.

"But I'm sorry. Please don't hate me forever. I'm sorry I made a mistake. I'm stupid, I'm dumb, but I'am sorry. He loosened his grip on her wrists, and put her down. He pulled her closer to him. She cried on his chest. Still lightly pounding her fist. "I hate you," she cried. "I know Zoe. I fucked up." He lifted her head and looked into her eyes. "I'm sorry Zoey. I made a mistake." He kissed her lips softly. "Please just give me one more chance. I'm sorry." He leaned down and kissed her again.

Zoey tried to push him away, but he held her tight. "No I'm not letting you leave me. You can't leave me babe. Please! I need you... I love you." Zoey tried to put some distance between them. " Just Stop fucking talking David! You don't mean shit that you're saying, so just stop! Let me go and I swear I'll let you go. Just forget me!" " No I'm not letting go!" He grabbed her arm and pulled her to him. You're mine! You were made for me." He kissed her hard and passionate, then reached under the over sized t-shirt, and pulled her panties down.

"David stop!" Zoey grabbed a hold to her lace panties. "No! I don't want too! You know you don't want me too either!" He yanked her panties one good time, and they fell to the floor. David kissed her again. "I was stupid. I'm sorry." He said through kisses. Zoey continued to whimper, as he kissed her lips, neck, and face. "I love you Zoey you know I love you. I'm not letting you get rid of me."

She gripped a tight hold of his shirt, and kissed him back as hard as she could, both of them sucking in each other's air. Zoey gripped the back of his neck and pulled him down further. They lied down onto the carpet. David lifted the t-shirt and let his hands roam all over her body. He sucked her neck and began working his way down to her breast. He ran his tongue around her areola, and then he sucked her hard nipples.

David went back, and forth between the left, and right breast sucking, biting, and teasing them both. He kissed her stomach and then continued down to her thighs. He spread her legs apart and held them in place, while he kissed, licked, and sucked her vagina slowly. Zoey reached down and griped the back of his neck. She spread her legs apart some more, while moving her vagina to meet each stroke of his tongue, grinding harder and harder.

"I fucking hate you!" She called out before pushing his head away. Zoey got up and pushed his back against the floor. "Take these fucking clothes off!" She demanded. David lifted his arms, as she pulled his shirt over his head. Zoey undid his belt, pulling off his denim jeans, as well as his boxers. She threw them to the other side of the room, before grabbing his hard penis between both her hands, and easing her way down on to it.

Zoey eased him inside of her, until her juices and vagina lips fully covered his penis. " Ahh" she moaned out in both pain, and pleasure, as she felt the head of his penis deep inside of her. Zoey was so angry she didn't even complain. She needed this, she had so much anger and frustration built up, and now she finally had the chance to release it. Zoey dug her nails into his chest, as she held her head back, and bounced up and down on his dick.

David held on to her waist, while looking down, watching his dick move in and out of her pink wet walls.

The vein in his Penis throbbed each time she went up and then down. Zoey continued to ride him, grinding harder and harder, her juices seeping from her vagina, drenching his midsection, and balls. "I hate you! I fucking hate you David!" She continued to scream out, as she cried.

"You don't hate me. You love me." David flipped her over onto her stomach, spread her legs, and entered her wet pussy from behind. He cupped his hands over hers, as she dug into the carpet. "If you hate me so much then why is my dick in you huh?" He whispered, as he pushed deep inside of her, causing her to scream out. "Fuck you David! I do hate you!" David pushed deeper inside of her. "So you don't love me Zoe?"

A rush of warm juices squirted from her vagina. "Stop lying. You do love me. Do you still love me?" He whispered into her ear. Zoey bit down on her lip and dug her nails deeper into the carpet, as she arched her back and held her head down. Zoey was trying her hardest to hold out. "You know you still love me baby. You already came on this dick, just tell me you still love me. Tell me this is still my pussy, and you ain't give it away."

David went in and out of her, stroking her walls, and then pushing deep inside of her. Zoey unable to hold out any longer whispered, "I still love you. I still love you, babe it's yours." They locked lips, and kissed roughly, as David stroked faster and faster. Zoey squeezed her pussy muscles tighter, until she felt a jerk inside of her. David's warm cum shot out, and filled her insides. He collapsed on top of her.

Zoey still clenched her muscles tight, as his penis still throbbed, then slowly went limp. David pulled her hair from her face and kissed her eyelids. Followed by her forehead. "I love you." Zoey smiled. "I love you too. Now get off of me. You know I hate all that mushy shit!" Zoey said sticking out her tongue. David smirked, and then slapped her playfully across her ass, before pushing himself up from the floor.

CHAPTER EIGHT

Birthday Suit

Bryce lay slumped across his long sectional, watching his brand new 70" inch television. A case of beer sat on the white plush carpet beneath his feet. Two remote controls lay in his lap. One was for the television and another for the cable. In his hand he gripped an ice-cold beer, which dripped water onto the carpet. If his wife were home to see him at this very moment she would be raising all kinds of hell.

Honestly on any other day Bryce would comply with her demands, but today wasn't just any other day. Today was Bryce's birthday. He could careless about her neat freak bullshit. Today was his day, and if he wanted to kick his feet up, and make a mess in his living room, then so be it. All he needed was some hot wings, a few of his boys over to join in and watch the game with him, and his night would be complete. But no, instead his wife arranged for a car to be sent for him around 7 o'clock for this big fancy dinner.

This required him to get all dressed up, and pretend as

though he liked her uptight, snotty, corny joke telling ass coworkers. Bryce took a swig from his beer, and then glanced at his watch. "Damn 6pm already!" He said out loud, as he sucked his teeth. Bryce really did not feel like going to this event. He loved his wife with all his heart. Any man would be a fool not too. She was intelligent, sophisticated, caring, and drop dead gorgeous.

She could easily stand next to any model, or actress, and give them a run for their money. Not too mention she made him laugh. With all this being said you would think, that someone as wonderful as her would have much nicer, down to earth friends. "Wrong!" Bryce said aloud, as he took another swig from his beer. Ever since his wife had gotten this new promotion, he hasn't seen much of her. She was always swamped with work and she hasn't been much fun lately.

He sat there shaking his head. Bryce worked just as hard as his wife Lauren. The only difference is, he always made time for her, and he damn sure wasn't boring. Just when he was making up his mind to skip the whole thing, His cell phone began to ring. Bryce looked down, and saw his wife's name appear across the screen. He sucked his teeth. Bryce briefly prepped the excuse he would give her, as to why he would not be attending the festivities.

He quickly answered the call. Bryce could barely get a hello out of his mouth. Lauren wasted no time spitting her demands. "Honey please tell me that you are not still in your boxers! Lounging around! The car service is scheduled for 8pm. I just finished confirming it. Please arrive on time honey. Please! Please! Please! This dinner is very important to me! Oh, and one last thing! Make sure you wear one of your best suits!" She ended the call abruptly.

Bryce removed the phone from his ear and stared at it. He couldn't believe that, he didn't get a chance to get not one word in. He threw his phone down beside him and put his head back. He covered his face with both of his hands. Bryce let out a loud grunt, before pushing himself up from the couch. He Slowly made his way towards the master bedroom. Bryce walked towards the right side of the room, where his closet was located, opposite from his wife's.

He walked inside. The walls were covered with large floor mirrors, and the floor was covered in carpet. About one hundred suits were neatly hung above rows of shoes and sneakers of all styles. Some of them were leather, some suede, some sporty, some comfy, you name it he had them. On the opposite side of the suits was a wall of neatly stacked rows of denim jeans, sweat suits, tracksuits, fitted hats, and a whole bunch of street attire.

Directly in the middle of the large closet was a wide rotating dresser, which held all his jewelry, smell goods, and under clothes. Bryce walked over to it and leaned against it. Bryce stood there pondering what to wear. He ended up opting for a pair of leather shoes, and a brand new suit he had tailored for himself last month. The suit had yet to even be removed from the plastic. What better occasion than now he thought, as he grabbed the suit, and placed it on a wall hook.

Bryce stripped down, and headed for the shower. About an hour or so later he stood in front of the mirror, looking as though he was about to do a photo shoot for GQ magazine. He looked damn good. Although he didn't feel like going out; looking good made him feel damn good.

He looked down at his gold watch that now read 7:45pm. "Damn it's almost about that time already!" Bryce said aloud. He grabbed one of his trench coats, and draped it over his arm.

He was about to sit back in front of his flat screen, when his doorman buzzed the intercom, letting him know the car service had arrived. Bryce grabbed his phone, and leather wallet. He headed for the door. Once down stairs a black limo with dark tinted windows waited for him. The driver held the door open for him to get in. Bryce could tell from the pecan colored seats, that this was not their usual limo service, Him and Lauren often used for events.

He quickly got in and laid his coat next to him. His eyes roamed the insides of the limo. There were two flat screen televisions, LED lighting lined throughout, and a mini bar directly in the middle. A bottle of his favorite cognac sat in a bucket of ice. Bryce was definitely impressed. His wife always had excellent taste, so he wasn't surprised that she went all out. However he was taken aback slightly. He reached for the bottle and poured himself a drink.

Bryce considered mixing it down, but decided against it. He figured if he was going to put up with Lauren's snobby ass coworkers; he might as well have some kind of liquor in his system. " I'm the birthday boy! I might as well enjoy myself a little!" He quickly threw back the drink, and then poured himself another. Bryce was already in a better mood by his third glass. He glanced down at his watch. They had been riding for about 40 minutes now.

Where the hell was this damn event taking place? He thought. Before Bryce could even get the chance to ask the driver if they were almost there. The limo began to slow down. The Limo came to a complete stop. He could hear the driver taking off his seat belt. Bryce took this time to check his reflection in the mirror and pop a mint in his mouth. The driver opened the door for him. He collected his things, and stepped out.

Bryce nearly stumbled out. He laughed to himself. " I've had one too many drinks," He said, while quickly smoothing out his suit, and looking around. He didn't know where the hell he was. Bryce was expecting this event to take place at a hotel in the city, or somewhere extravagant as always. Instead he was somewhere in the village, or somewhere way downtown Manhattan, or so it looked. People walked the streets in sets of two, and groups of four & six.

There were quite a few bars, pubs, Restaurants, and tattoo parlors on both sides of the block. Bryce turned to his driver with a confused look across his face. This was some mistake. He must have taken a wrong turn, or something of that nature. To Bryce's surprise his driver closed the door. He began to usher Bryce towards this large black door. It looked as though it weighed a ton. The driver walked over to it and pounded three heavy knocks with his fist, and then quickly ran back over to the limo and got in, without uttering a word.

Bryce stood there confused as. He was about to dial his wife's cell phone number, but stopped once he heard what sounded like locks being unlocked. The big door opened a bit. There stood two beautiful women. One was a blonde and the other a Brunette. One had blue eyes, and the other had green. Both women were dressed in sexy lingerie and heels. Bryce was taken aback again. *Where the hell did his driver mistakenly drop him?* He thought.

Neither of the women said a word to him. Instead they

just stepped aside, gesturing for him to come in. Bryce looked around, as though they were motioning towards someone else, but there was no one else there. His husband instinct immediately kicked in. His instincts were telling him he should back away, and call his wife. Something wasn't adding up. He needed to reach out to Lauren, so he could find out what was going on. However the male temptation inside of him was saying something else.

Suddenly he had to use the restroom awfully bad, or maybe his mind was just playing tricks with his bladder. Shortly after he got this urge to urinate, his mind began to come up with reasons why, it would be a good idea, for him to follow the two women inside. Bryce loosened his belt buckle slightly, as some sort of attempt to make himself not want to use the bathroom. He began tapping his pants, and coat pocket in search of his cell phone.

Bryce had to call Lauren. She would kill him if he went inside this place. Females were half naked, him dressed to kill, and intoxicated on top of all that. "No way, no thanks!" He said backing away and attempting to dial Lauren's number. Bryce stopped in mid dial, when both women said at the same time " we have been awaiting you mr. Dunning" Both in sync, as though they were Charlie's Angels, or some shit.

He hit end on the phone call. " Excuse me. What did you say?" Bruce moved closer to make sure, that he had heard both women say his last name. "We have been awaiting you Mr. Dunning!" Both women repeated once more. This time the blonde reached out and gripped his wrist. Caught completely off guard Bryce allowed the women to lure him in. Once inside the place he began to squint slightly, because the place was so dimly lit.

If Bryce wasn't mistaken it seemed, as though smoke filled the air just a little. A thick fancy white carpet covered the floors. There were tables, private booths also white in color, with leather seating. The booths were scattered throughout the place. From what Bryce could see there were other people in the place. This put him at ease just a little. At least now he knew these women weren't trying to rob him, or set him up. At least not with these other people around as witnesses.

The Brunette reached out and grabbed his hand; snapping him out of his gaze. "Can I take your coat Mr. Dunning?" "No! That won't be necessary. In fact I'm not staying! This must be some mistake. I was suppose to be meeting my wife for a dinner, which is being held by the company she works for." The little brunette began to pout. "Aww that's such a pity. I was hoping..." "We were hoping." Said the blonde joining in. "We were hoping that you would like what you see here, and consider eating with us instead."

Both women leaned against him. The blonde pressed her body against his so tightly; he could feel her hard nipples through his shirt. Bryce took a deep breath. "You are going to walk out of here Bryce Dunning, and go call your beautiful wife." He kept saying over, and over to himself. Right in mid thought the brunette leaned in closer. In one swift motion she reached down and caressed his midsection.

Bryce stared at her. Completely shocked by her boldness, but completely aroused, and turned on at the same time. He could feel his penis begin to stiffen. "Where's your restroom?' He asked abruptly." She smiled.

"Right this way." Both females said at the same time. As they made their way to the restroom, they passed several other beautiful females some topless, some clothed, and others completely in the nude.

The females did not hesitate to walk right up to Bryce, and touch, wink, and blow kisses. One of them even walked up to him and gripped his penis. "Would you like us to come in with you?" said both women. Each of them held a pleading look in their eyes. "No I think I'll be able to manage just fine!" Replied Bryce "Awe that's too bad. We'll be right out here waiting for you Mr. Dunning." Bryce turned to enter the restroom.

As he was going in, two gorgeous women were escorting out a young man, one on each of his arms. The man had the biggest smile on his face. Bryce went straight to a stall and relieved himself. Then he walked over to the sink to splash some water on his face. Bryce had to make sure he was really awake. His wife was going to kill him. He reached into his coat pocket for his cell phone. To his surprise there was only two missed calls from Lauren.

Usually there would be at least five missed calls and at least one 10-page text message. Bryce unlocked his phone to call Lauren to explain the mix up, but before the phone could ring once on the other end, the Blonde grabbed his cell phone from his hand, and ended the call. " Sorry big boy no outside calls! Especially not to the misses." She said looking at the phone. "Follow Us." Each woman took one of his wrists and pulled him towards the door.

They lead him down this long narrow hallway with blue LED lighting to light the way. A large part of Bryce wanted to just ask the women to release him, so he could get the hell out of there, but there was this little piece of him that wanted to stay. Lauren and him had been married for a little over 8years. In those 8 years Bryce has never once cheated on her, but then again he has never allowed himself to get into a situation like this one.

He had a thousand thoughts running through his head. You would think that 8 years of marriage would have been enough for him to turn around and leave, but it wasn't. That little piece of him that wanted to stay was beginning to spread like a disease. His curiosity and the temptation of having those women, at his beck and call was eating him up, and getting the best of him. Once they made it to the end of the hallway, they made a left, then walked through these thick velvet curtains.

Behind the curtains there was a private section, the decor was still the same; however there was a long stage in the middle of the room. The same blue colored LED lighting from the halls lined the stage. It also glowed underneath the seating and tables. It was pretty much the only light in the room. The females walked Bryce over to a table, which was positioned directly in front of the stage.

On the table sat a bucket of ice with glasses, and two bottles of his favorite cognac. Without asking both women began removing his coat from his shoulders. The brunette draped his trench coat over the chair, while the blonde grasped his wrist, and pulled him down into the chair. The blonde immediately applied pressure to the right side of his body, by wrapping one of her legs over his, and leaning her upper body against part of his chest and shoulder blade.

"Let us pour you a drink." She whispered in his ear, before he could object the brunette was already bringing the glass towards his lips, almost forcing him to take a sip.

Bryce then took a deep breath and devoured the entire drink. He wiped his mouth on the wrist part of his blazer, then handed the brunette back the glass. "More!" He said in a hurried tone. He put the second glass to his lips and threw its contents back as well.

He slammed the glass down on the table, causing it to shake a bit. The brunette was now sitting on his left side, positioned the same way the blonde was, both women began to kiss, and suck his earlobes. They each helped to get him out of his blazer. The women then took turns unbuttoning his shirt. Bryce's head was telling him he should leave, but his feet were planted flat to the floor. His body felt so relaxed, numb even.

His heart was beating so fast. Bryce was certain it would jump right out of his chest at any given moment. The blonde began to kiss on his neck, and work her way down to his chest, but Bryce quickly stopped her. He wasn't going to let things get that out of hand, but as he was trying to stop the Blonde from going any further. The brunette joined in, between both of their soft lips, wet kisses, and the sensation they were giving his body.

It was almost impossible for him not to give in. He was so wrapped up in what was taking place on his lap; he didn't even notice that there were three females dancing on the stage in front of him. All three of them were masked, making it extremely hard for him to see their faces. As creepy as this should have been to Bryce, It wasn't. The women being masked were a complete turn on for him.

All three of the females were nicely shaped, and around the same size. One of them had the nicest ass he had ever seen. When she began to make it bounce up and down, his dick began to stiffen immediately. One of the other two Females on the stage had some sexy lips and a long tongue. She had no shame using it to lick and suck the breast of the other female who had the nice ass. The third female continued to dance in the most seductive manner.

Bryce couldn't see her face, but he could tell that she was gorgeous. She had some of the most beautiful legs. Bryce could say they were the most sexist he has ever seen, but then he would be lying, because his wife's legs were just as irresistible. All though the blonde, and brunette were going to work kissing, licking, and massage his chest. The woman with the nice legs had his full attention. He stared at her thinking so many inappropriate thoughts.

She continued to dance for him like there was no other person in the room, but the two of them. The other two masked females began to make their way off the stage. They strutted down to where he was sitting. The female with the nice ass positioned herself right in front of him. She bent over, and laid her palms flat on the table. She turned and looked back at him, as she made her ass cheeks clap for him. The female with the long tongue reached out, and grabbed his hand.

She placed it on the ass of the other female leaning over the table. Bryce palmed the female's ass, and then he gripped it tightly. His dick was now so hard. There was no way in hell he could hide, or suppress his erection. The female noticed his erection right away. She smiled devilishly, and then she stopped her little ass clapping routine. She took a seat on Bryce's lap. She began to grind slowly on Bryce's dick.

Bryce took his hands, and ran them down the female's bare back. He then placed them on her waist. He helped her move her waistline to a slow Rhythm on his penis. The female with the sexy lips and long tongue was now repositioned in front of the female on his lap. She was licking the insides of her thighs. The blonde, and brunette were beside him on top of one another kissing, licking and sucking one another's body. The third female was no longer dancing for him on the stage.

Bryce looked around quickly. She was not in the room anymore. At least she wasn't within eyesight. Bryce didn't have much time to be worried about her anyways. He had so much going on in his lap. Before Bryce could have another complete thought; in one swift motion the woman grinding on top of him did a 360 spin. She was now facing him. She positioned herself on her knees. On the exact same side where the brunette once was.

The sexy lipped female followed suite, and positioned herself the same way, but on the opposite side, where the blonde once sat. The female with the nice ass grasped one of her breast, and brought it to his mouth. Her hard nipple brushed across his lips. She urged him to lick them; as much as Bryce wanted to he just couldn't bring himself to do it. He bit down on his bottom lip instead. However the female was persistent. She signaled to the female opposite her.

Both females moved closer to one another, and began to kiss each other passionately in front of him. Bryce reached down and grasped his stiff penis, as he continued to watch the four females around him go at each other. With his other hand he reached up, and attempted to remove the mask from one of the females faces. Bryce just had to see how they looked underneath it, with bodies as gorgeous as theirs, he was sure there faces had to be equally beautiful.

His curiosity was at an all time high, but before he could get a chance to pull the mask back, the female with the nice lips grasped his hand; she took one of his fingers into her mouth nice and slow. The inside of her mouth was nice and moist. Her lips were, plump, soft, and the perfect shade of pink. Bryce couldn't help but imagine his hard penis moving in and out of them. He worked his finger in and out of her mouth imagining her sucking his penis with those lips of hers.

Without warning the other female forcefully gripped his belt buckle. Bryce put his hand over hers and tried to remove it. Although he was intoxicated he still had some of his senses and some strength left. All of that drained from his body, when the other female reached over, simply unzipping his pants, and pulling the head of his penis out. She took that long tongue of hers, and ran it over the tip of his hard dick. She sucked up the small amounts of pre-cum that was escaping from it.

"Ahhhh shit!" Bryce said aloud with his head back. His eyes were fixed on the ceiling. His grip on the other female's hand began to loosen. She took this opportunity to quickly undo his belt all the way. Both females helped each other, so they could slide his pants and underwear off midway. The female licking the head of his penis slowly proceeded to put his entire penis into her mouth. Within seconds it was covered in her saliva.

The other female with the nice behind got down on her knees beside the other woman. Both women took turns licking, and sucking his penis. One gently sucked and licked his balls, while the other kept his shaft nice and wet. Every few moments they would briefly stop and kiss, as well as suck each other's face, and lips. Bryce couldn't believe this shit. Just an hour ago he was on his way to a boring ass business event.

Now here he was getting the best blow-job of his entire life. Not by one but two beautiful females. He looked to the left of him. The blonde, and the brunette were now in the sixty-nine position pleasuring one another with their tongues. He looked down at the two females that were sucking the life out of his dick. They both stared back at him with their lips wet and mouths full. Bryce looked away; he didn't want to cum just yet, he was enjoying himself way too much.

He put his head back and closed his eyes this time. The only thing he could hear was slurping sounds and lip smacking from the two women on their knees. He could also hear the moaning sounds from the other two females pleasing each other. Bryce listened on in complete bliss. Suddenly all the noise seized. He looked down. The two females had stopped sucking his penis. They were now smiling up at him. Both women kissed the head of his penis, then got up to leave.

The blonde, and brunette were already out of sight. Bryce was confused. He was about to pull his pants up, when a hand gripped his shoulders from behind. Bryce quickly looked behind him. There stood the third woman with the nice legs. The same woman who danced on the stage earlier, that he couldn't keep his eyes off of. Bryce didn't get a chance to say anything to her, because she quickly put a blindfold over his eyes.

Bryce's body began to tense up and he started to mouthed obscenities. He immediately relaxed once she put her finger over his mouth, and told him to hush. The female then took his hand and rubbed it up her nice smooth legs. Bryce licked his lips. His penis was still hard as ever. Nice legs had always been a turn on for him. If only he could see her face. He thought to himself. Now that he was blind folded he was even more anxious and curious than before.

The female straddled his lap and began kissing his neck, and nibbling on his ear. The female was pleasuring his g-spot dead on. She rubbed her ass on his stiff penis. She then slyly attempted to undo the buttons to his shirt, but again Bryce resisted. There was no way he was going any further. He had already allowed these women to pleasure him orally. He wouldn't dear go any further. The female smiled to herself, and continued to work her hips. She went right back to foraying his g-spot.

The female stopped short trying to slow her own breathing, before continuing. She could no longer hold out herself. She leaned in real close to his ear. She whispered "Happy Birthday". Bryce's entire body went numb, its almost as if all the blood left his body, along with all the liquor he had consumed in the past few hours. He quickly removed his blindfold. He stood face to face with his wife Lauren.

His heart beat wildly in his chest. Bryce was certain that he was going to past out any moment. He didn't know what the hell was going on. For sure he thought he was dreaming, or being set up, but surprisingly his wife wasn't angry or furious. He looked up at the mask sitting on top of her head, then down at the lingerie that barely covered her body. That's when he began to realize, that she had been the third girl dancing on the stage, and that this was indeed a set up, just not the kind of life threatening set up he was thinking of.

Bryce suddenly felt very stupid. He should have known something was up from the beginning. How silly of him not to know that this was entirely his wife's doing. Before Bryce could have yet another panicked fearful thought. Lauren leaned in and kissed him passionately. "Happy Birthday." She whispered in between kisses. Bryce began to kiss her back, more out of fear than anything. Lauren begins to help him get completely undressed.

Bryce couldn't keep his hands and lips off of her. He gripped a handful of her hair and pulled her lips back to his. He stuck his tongue deep into her mouth. " My gosh I fucking love you for this! I should have known you had something up your sleeves," Bryce said planting yet another sloppy wet kiss on her lips, and pointing his index finger into her face. "Oh you love me huh? You didn't even get the full surprise, and you already love me, maybe I should just stop now then." Lauren said biting down on his bottom lip.

"Woman don't you dare hold out on me." Bryce said, while putting his hand around her neck, pulling her mouth back to his. Lauren gripped his ears as they engaged in yet another kiss. "Just know I do love you." She whispered, before turning around and doing some sort of hand gesture, which Bryce couldn't make out. The female with the blonde hair, and the one with the nice ass that he couldn't take his eyes off of reappeared. "Guess who we get to put on a show for?" Lauren asked with a devilish grin on her face.

Bryce laughed "Really you're going to let them watch?" Bryce was hoping for a three some, but he didn't mind settling for the two women watching him put his thing down. At this point he would have settled for anything his wife proposed, after all that just went down, only moments ago. Plus he knew she was always against sharing him with anyone else, so this was definitely a big step on her behalf. Bryce quickly began to get out of whatever was left of his clothing.

The women got up, and came closer, so close that they were now within arms reach. Bryce wasn't expecting them to be this close, but he was beyond happy that they did decide to get closer. This sure as hell increased his chances of the women joining in on the action. Bryce laid down on the couch. He then reached out for Lauren's wrist. He pulled her on to his face. Bryce wasted no time pushing his tongue deep inside of Lauren's pink vagina walls.

Lauren reached down and gripped a hold of her husband's ears. She moved her hips to the rhythm of his tongue. Lauren stood up on her feet in a squatting position, but she was still over Bryce's face. She slowly rocked her body back and forth, as though she was riding some kind of wave. Each time she rocked she could feel Bryce's tongue lick her clitoris, along with her pussy lips, and her ass. Lauren put her head back and rocked faster.

Bryce stiffened his tongue as much as he could and continued to match her every move. He could hear Lauren moaning his name loudly. He knew that in any moment she was going to climax. Bryce reached up and gripped her thighs. Pushing her downward on to his tongue. Bryce licked, and sucked her clitoris, lips, and walls. He didn't slow down, until he felt her juices dripping down his chin. He sucked and slurped trying not to let anymore go to waste.

Lauren jerked, and squirmed on top of his face. Bryce could care less; he wasn't letting her go, until she released every drop. Once Lauren stopped shaking and moving, Bryce let her get up. Lauren was about to straddle him, when Bryce quickly jumped up. He was not about to let his wife ride him. He did not want to cum just yet. He knew if he let Lauren get on top she would definitely get the job done.

Bryce stood up, his mouth still covered in Lauren's juices slightly. He pulled Lauren towards him and planted a wet kiss on her lips. Lauren took her tongue and traced the outline of his lips, getting a taste of her own juices. "I love you." She whispered. Bryce griped her waist, and the back of her neck. He turned Lauren around, making her bend over the leather chair. Bryce planted kisses down her back.

He ran the head of his penis back and forth between her pussy lips. Lauren bit down on her bottom lip. She loved when her husband would tease her like this; it sent her sex drive through the roof. Bryce glanced back at the two females. Both still looked on while pleasuring one another with their fingers. Bryce grinned to himself like a kid in a toy store. He turned his attention back to his wife.

Bryce angled her body slightly to the side, so that the females could get a good look at his penis, stroking Lauren's insides. Without warning he pushed his hard penis inside of Lauren's vagina opening, causing her to dig her nails into the leather chair. Bryce went in and out of her slowly at first, letting Lauren's juices moisten his penis. He pulled out and stroked his dick with his hand, making sure that every inch was covered in her wetness. He then shoved his stiff penis back inside of her.

Bryce began to move in and out of her at a faster pace. He dug his fingers into her ass cheeks, as he pumped in and out of her. Each time he pushed himself deep inside Lauren's walls, she cried out. Bryce could feel himself about to cum. He quickly slowed his pace, and pulled out. His penis fell between his thighs. He bent down and sucked Lauren's pussy lips, then parted them with his tongue, slowly running it from her clitoris all the way back to her ass crack. Lauren turned her head, and shot him a look, that let him know he had enticed her entire soul.

At that point Bryce didn't even bother to put on a show any longer. He knew he had pleased his wife many times over. Now it was time he sit back, and let her bring the show, which she had started to an end. He bent down and licked her ass crack once more, then blew on it, teasing her one last time. Lauren's body tensed up, as she giggled at the feeling her husband's lips left behind. "Ok Mr! That's enough!"

Lauren turned around and pushed Bryce down on the chair. "My turn." She whispered into his ear. She then slid down and planted a wet kiss on the head of his penis. Lauren licked around the head of it before taking it all into her mouth. She eased his penis inside until it hit the back of her throat. Lauren didn't stop until his entire shaft was moistened again. Lauren stood up and climbed on top of his lap. She put both of her hands on his shoulders for extra support, as she squatted over his penis. Lauren reached down, and gripped it, as she guided it through her wet pink walls.

Lauren wasted no time slowly bouncing up and down on top of his stiff penis. She was careful to keep it inserted as she increased her pace and force. Lauren's juices were flowing freely again, slowly seeping down his shaft, and nut sack. Bryce put both his hands over his face and laid his head back towards the ceiling. Lauren Knew he was about to climax any second now. She quickly signaled to the females behind her, while keeping her same rhythm, so not to alarm Bryce of the final trick she had up her sleeve.

She wanted him to be in complete shock. As soon as Bryce abruptly removed his hands from his face revealing this wild look in his eyes, Lauren knew she had accomplished just that. He was shocked. Bryce looked down beneath him. Both women were at his feet down on all fours. They began to suck, and lick the cum, which seeped from Lauren's pussy off of his thighs, and nut sack. Lauren still continued to bounce up, and down on his shaft, while all of this was going on.

Bryce was in disbelief. He couldn't believe this was actually taking place. He didn't want to cum, but he couldn't hold out any longer. Especially not with the way Lauren was riding his dick. Perfection would be an understatement. Bryce could feel himself about to explode. Right when his semen was about to shoot out from his rock hard penis Lauren quickly jumped off of him. In one swift motion miss big booty grabbed his penis, taking it into her mouth.

Bryce's semen quickly filled the back of her throat. Bryce gripped the back of her head. He held it in place until he released himself. Once he loosened his grip she swallowed and smiled up at him. The blonde quickly took hold of his penis and began to jerk whatever was left of his semen into her mouth. Bryce looked on in awe, secretly wishing he had more semen to put down her throat, but they had devoured every bit of it, along with his energy. Bryce's entire body fell limp included his penis.

The females said their goodbyes by kissing the head of

his penis. Once they left Lauren inched herself back over to her husband. She mounted him once more. Bryce laid there in his birthday suit spent, intoxicated, and covered in sweat. Lauren leaned in and planted a wet kiss to his forehead. "Happy Birthday." She whispered to him.

CHAPTER NINE
Twining

India had been sitting at the bar for the past hour. She was now on her third drink. India waved the bar tender over, who quickly hurried in her direction. India had never seen him here before, not ever, but then again she hasn't attended this lounge in quite some time. India use to be a regular at this place. She stopped attending as much, because she hated being around people in her work suits, while everyone else around her looked all fancy and dolled up.

The bartender was a young guy; he looked like he was in his early twenties. He was probably a college student trying to make some extra cash, or maybe cool with the owner or something like that. India quickly dismissed her thoughts once he approached her. "What can I get you ma'am?" He asked in a polite tone. "I'll take another." India said motioning towards her glass. "Yes right away ma'am!" He hurried to the other end of the bar to make her drink, then quickly returning with it. He placed it in front of her with fresh napkins, and then slipped two

4 Head Kissers Short Erotic Tales

straws inside.

India immediately tossed the straws to the side and began to down the drink in big gulps. A bar was the last place she needed to be right about now. India had one of the worst days ever at her job of 10 years. The drinks she was consuming, were giving her the firepower she needed to call her boss up right then and there. India wanted to tell his old ass to go straight to hell and to kiss her ass. She chuckled a bit at her own thoughts. "The old pervert probably would enjoy that." She said aloud, while moving the ice around in her drink.

The more she kept thinking about the old fart the more vexed she became, the more drinks she ordered. A few hours had passed now. India still sat at the bar. However she was no longer sitting up, she was leaning over a bit. Her cell phone and clutch sat off to the side of her. All the people had already stumbled out of the establishment in two's and groups of fours. The young bartender called out to her. "Ma'am are you okay?" India fanned his question off.

"Ma'am we are closing up. Is there anything I can get you?" India didn't bother to respond this time. The young bartender walked over to her and placed his hand over hers. "Ma'am are you okay? Would you like me to call for help?" India slowly lifted her head up. "No that's ok! I'm fine." She smiled up at him and tapped his hand. She reached for her cell phone, to see if she could get in touch with her driver. India should have been given him a call, to let him know she would be in need of his services tonight, but she had forgot.

She was so wrapped up in the events of her awful day it slipped her mind. India scrolled through her call log until she found his number. She decided she was going to call him anyways. There was no way she was driving home in her condition. He picked up on the third ring. "Hey john... sorry to call you on such short notice, but I need you." She listened to the voice on the other end. "Ok so how long before you reach me?" She paused to listen again.

India let out a deep sigh, "Okay I guess I'll just have to wait." She dictated the address to him before she hung up. India then dug into her clutch and peeled off two crisp hundred-dollar bills, she slipped it under her empty glass. She flipped open her compact mirror, quickly checking her hair, and makeup before leaving. "Are you sure you're going to be okay ma'am?" "Yes Dylan!" She said squinting to read the small name tag, he had pinned to his white button up.

"I'll be just fine honey. I have someone coming to pick me up. Thanks for everything. Oh by the way I left one of those bills for you." India winked at him. She then swung her suit blazer behind one of her shoulders, and proceeded towards the revolving doors. "Hey ma'am!" Dylan called after her. India turned her head slightly. "Thank you!" He flashed a perfect white smile, revealing deep dimples on both sides of his cheeks.

India smiled, but said nothing, instead continuing towards the doors. She wobbled slightly in her heels, but for the most part she was ok. Her whole body felt warm and relaxed. She hadn't been this buzzed in awhile, she rarely ever went out anymore or dated, because she spent so much time at work. Instead of feeling 35 she felt twice her age. Once outside in the fresh air, India took a seat off to the side, to wait on her driver.

She sat her clutch in her lap, and rested her head up against this giant cement pillar. India looked down at her watch. It was almost 2am. She shook her head, how the hell did she let herself get this carried away? She had been at the bar for nearly 4hours. "I hope John gets here soon." She said aloud, as she placed her hand over her mouth to cover it as she let out a yawn. India closed her eyes, but shortly after she was being shook awake. She opened her eyes slowly. Her eyelids felt heavy.

India could hear a male voice from a far. "See man I told you to leave that damn woman alone! You always trying to save some damn body!" "Would you shut up, and let me make sure she's okay!" "Ma'am are you ok?" "Dee man she's alive! Now Let's go!" "Hold on I need to make sure she's ok!" India opened her eyes fully. She thought she was seeing double and she really was. There stood the young bar tender that waited on her all evening, along with another young man, that looked identical to him.

India looked around, she must have fell asleep. She immediately felt embarrassed. "I'm fine. Thank you. I'm just a little..." She yawned "Sleepy," She said slipping her arms through her suit blazer. "Thanks so much Dylan for asking. Very polite of you." Dylan flashed his perfect white smile, again revealing his dimples. "You remembered my name." He said, excitement dripping from his words. India blushed a little.

She did in fact remember his name. In fact as much as she hated to admit it, his politeness, and coy demeanor was such a turn on for her. She cleared her throat, but said nothing. Instead she looked at her watch, and then past him. Her driver John was nowhere in sight! Dylan noticed her eyes darting back and forth, as if she were searching for something. "Are you waiting for someone?" Dylan asked. "Yeah I was." She said, slipping her clutch underneath her arm, and getting up from where she was sitting. "Now I'm just going to catch a cab."

"A cab! I can't let you do that. How far do you live from here? I can give you a ride." Before India could respond. The young man who looked just like Dylan began to yell out to him again. "Dee man I'm bout to leave your ass! Come on! I want go home and eat!" Dylan turned to hush his brother. "Ryan could you relax! Give me a minute! I'm sorry ma'am where is it you said you live?" India pushed her hair out of her face.

"Don't worry about it. I'll be ok. Thank you very much though." She turned to leave. Dylan reached out and grabbed her elbow. "With all do respect ma'am, but I don't think it's a good idea for you to go home alone. Let me give you a lift. I promise you I'm a good guy." Dylan flashed that smile of his again, but this time he didn't look away. He bit down on his bottom lip, staring India straight in the eyes, undressing her with his.

India began to fidget a bit. She looked around for her driver, still no sight of him. "Ok I'll let you drop me home, I'll just send for my car first thing tomorrow morning." Dylan smiled. "I'm glad you are going to let me take you home. Oh and don't mind my brother, he can be so rude at times." India smiled at him. "I can see! I'm not afraid though!" She said peering over his shoulder, taking a look at Ryan. Dylan held his arm out to lead the way. India put her arm in his; she followed him towards the car.

"Ryan this is India. India this is my rude twin brother Ryan." Dylan said introducing the two. "Hi nice to meet you Ryan" India said holding out her hand, which Ryan embraced, then brought up to his lips, kissing the back of her hand in a cool slick way. "Nice to meet you. Everybody calls me Rye." Ryan said smirking. Dylan reached in and knocked his hand away. "Man would you cut it out! She doesn't want your crusty ass lips all over her!" Ryan laughed.

" And how would you know? It's not like she stopped me." Ryan winked at India. India couldn't help but chuckle a bit at his bluntness, and their little bickering over her; it kind of made her feel important. "See! Told you," shouted Ryan. "Whatever man lets go dweeb! The least you could do is get the door for her. Have you no manners," Dylan said to his brother with a disgusted look on his face. Ryan walked over to the car, he opened the door to the backseat, and let India get in.

Dylan walked over to the driver's side. Before he got in he signaled to his brother to get his attention. " I'm telling you now Rye man be on your best behavior!" Ryan looked at his brother and sucked his teeth. "Man leave me alone!" He said with an attitude. Dylan already knew, that what he said to his brother went in one ear, and out the other. As soon as they got in the car, Dylan didn't even get his seat belt on, or the car engine started, and his brother was already questioning India.

" So you a heavy drinker or something? You looked wasted back there." Ryan turned around in his seat, so he could watch India's reaction to his question. Dylan shook his head in disgust. He couldn't believe his brother asked her something like that. Dylan quickly shot him a dirty look before pulling off from the parking lot. India ran her tongue over her teeth and gums. She was becoming a little annoyed with Ryan. He thought he was so cool with his little sly remarks. India loved to teach guys like him valuable lessons.

She smirked a bit, as she cleared her throat to answer him! "Rye is it?" She said a bit sarcastically. " Indeed I was and still am a bit intoxicated, however the answer is no. I'm not a heavy drinker." " Could have fooled me!" Ryan said aloud. Dylan was about to speak up and address his brother's rudeness, but India quickly spoke up. She fired back a statement of her own. " And to think I thought you were the oldest of the two." She said, referring to both young men. "But judging by your rudeness, and lack of being able to hold your tongue, you quickly gave that up! Couldn't fool me for long."

India sat back in her seat and crossed her legs, hoping like hell she was correct, that Ryan was the youngest. Dylan chuckled a bit, giving it away that she was in fact correct. " See little brother I told you, that attitude of yours reveals your age every single time." Ryan sucked his teeth and waved off his brother's comment. Ryan directed his attention back to India. He couldn't even fake the fact that he was kind of taken aback by her sarcastic reply. Ryan didn't think she had it in her, being that She looked so sophisticated in her little suit and all.

Ryan was definitely turned on. He quickly cut his thoughts short, and turned around slightly in his seat, so that he could make eye contact. He cleared his throat before speaking." Last time I checked age wasn't nothing but a number doll." He said in a real slick & cool tone. Making sure to let each word slowly roll off his tongue. Indian shifted in her seat a bit, trying to hide the smirk that he put on her face. " I see you agree." Ryan said grinning.

India quickly suppressed her smirk. With a serious look on her face she replied flatly. "Maybe." Dylan peered at her through the rearview, and then he looked over at his brother. "Man would you leave the woman alone. She doesn't need your questioning." "Dylan would please just keep your eyes on the road. Miss lady is a grown woman. I'm sure if she couldn't handle my mouth she would say so." Ryan licked his lips, while looking Indian dead in her eyes, making it clear that he wanted her in the worst way.

Indian laughed at him, paying him absolutely no mind." How old are you guys anyways?" India asked, while giggling and stealing a sneak peek of Ryan's sexy lips. " Twenty one, but we will be twenty two!" They both replied in harmony. "Lawd you boys are just babies. What are you guys doing working at some damn bar? You need to have your butts in the books, or at an internship, getting some damn experience for the real world."

"Well last time I checked miss! Them books you speak of cost money, and I've never ran across a store that accepted experience, as a form of payment!" Ryan said sarcastically. Dylan quickly reached over and punched his brother in the arm. " Got damn it Ryan! Must you be a rude asshole all the time? You just can't turn it off can you?" Ryan laughed to himself. "Fine I won't say anything else for the rest of the drive!" Dylan sucked his teeth.

"I'm sorry Indian. I think what my brother was trying to say is, we really don't have any other choice, but to work. Our mother Passed giving birth to us, and our old man is sickly. We pretty much have to provide for one another." India pouted. " Wow that's so unfortunate. I'm extremely sorry I even asked." "Don't be! You didn't know." Said Dylan with his eyes fixed on the road. " So what about you miss lady? Got any kids, baby daddies, or any other habits we should know about?" asked Ryan.

Indian let out a fake laugh. " Very funny, but no. I do not have any kids, crazy boyfriends, or any other crazy drug habits." Dylan began to bring the car to a slow creep. " Which house is yours?" He asked. "That one all the way on the end." India used her Index finger to point her house out. "Damn miss that's a big ass house for one person. You living large!" Shouted Ryan. "Thank you, I always wanted a big house when I was a little girl."

" Well you damn sure accomplished that!" Ryan added in after she finished her statement. Dylan pulled his car right in front of the big house. "Whelp this is it." Said Dylan putting the car into park. " Thank you guys so very much for getting me home safe. I feel as though I should at least invite you guys in for a drink, or something, or maybe a tour of the place. I mean… I don't mean to be pushy, but I don't get many visitors." India paused and looked at the both of them.

" Shit you don't have to ask me twice!" Said Ryan Unhooking his seat belt. Dylan bust out with laughter. "Well I guess that's a yes India. We will come in and have a tour of your home. Do you mind if I pull up into the driveway?" "No. Not at all, go right ahead. It's not like my car is occupying it." Dylan pulled the car into the driveway and parked it. Each of them exited the vehicle. India leads the way.

As they walked towards the house, the pathway began to light up, underneath their feet. "Wow I'm really feeling these lights Miss! They are perfect for drunk nights." Said Ryan with a big smile across his face. " Why thank you." India said chuckling. " I installed them myself." " Wow

4 Head Kissers Short Erotic Tales

your beautiful and good with tools." Dylan chimed in. India smiled to herself, as she unlocked the huge front door.

"You guys have to leave your shoes in this area right here. There are no shoes allowed beyond this point." All of them took off their shoes and placed them on an antique looking rack. India already had a few pair of heels sitting on it. India continued on past the huge door way. She Grabbed both of the boys arms, pulling them into her living room, which was also her dining room, which also included a bar area.

She could see both of their eyes light up, just from looking at how high the ceilings were, from it hung a giant chandelier. The wooden floors had just been done, so the oversized genuine animal skin rug looked amazing on top of it. The highlight of this entire area of the house was, the white Grand piano, and the huge fireplace. The twins were so caught up in the interior design, they hadn't even noticed that India walked over to the bar, and popped the tops on two beers.

Ryan ran over to the Piano and rubbed his hand along the keys. " Miss You really must be making some bank! I can't believe you have a piano in your house. This is definitely some fly fancy shit." India smiled, as she walked over and handed each of them a beer. "Come on let me show you guys the pool. India leads them past the kitchen, and slid open a glass door, which lead to the back yard. India walked along the pool so that the lights surrounding it would come on.

" I must say your home is amazing Ms. India." Said Dylan, while taking a swig from his beer. "Oh stop with this Ms. Business. You guys are making me feel old. India will do just fine." They all laughed, " So India can we see the bedroom?" Asked Ryan jokingly. " Unfortunately guys the bedroom is a bit messy. I rather not take you guys up there." India giggled to herself. " Lets go back inside." India lead them back through the sliding glass door and over to the bar.

She was about to go get them both another beer, but then had a better idea. "Hey Ryan how about you work the bar. Dylan waited on me all night. Now it's your turn." Ryan laughed " Oh so you just going to put me to work huh? That's cool though. I don't mind waiting on you sexy lady." He grinned revealing his dimples that were almost identical to his brothers. It's just that Dylan's were much deeper. Actually their dimples and their personalities were the only way that you could tell them apart.

India took a seat by the bar. She tapped the bar stool next to her, indicating to Dylan she wanted him to take a seat. Ryan hopped his tall frame behind the bar. You would think he had been over before the way he maneuvered his way around. He opened up two more bottles of beer. He placed one in front of Dylan and one to the side for himself. Dylan shot Ryan a funny look, a look India couldn't quite make out, but she decided not to say anything. *Must be a twin thing* she thought.

About an hour or so pasted. They were still drinking and talking, but by now they had moved by the fireplace. Dylan sat on the sectional next to India, Ryan was laid out on the rug talking a whole bunch of nonsense, and cracking jokes. " Suddenly Dylan stood up holding his stomach. "I'm Sorry India, but may I please use your restroom? Between those beers, and all the appetizers I ate, while at work my stomach is doing flips." "Sure you can. You can use the one down in the guest area for your own privacy, and to save you some embarrassment in case," She paused. "Well you know."

" You mean in case he takes a crap, and blows up your bathroom!" blurted out Ryan. India tried to hold in her laughter, but with all the drinks she had consumed she couldn't. She fell back on to the sectional holding her stomach. Dylan stood there watching them both slightly annoyed, but he said nothing. Instead Dylan turned and walked down the long hallway, which lead to the other side of the house.

The guest area was damn near bigger than his entire apartment, which he shared with his brother and father. Dylan opened a few doors, popping his head in several rooms, until he came across the bathroom. Once he found it, he ran over to the sink, and splashed some water on his face. He had already consumed about four beers, beers that he shouldn't have accepted. Being that he was the one responsible for getting them home safely.

Dylan relieved himself, and then he washed his hands. He splashed some more water on his face. Dylan grabbed a small cup from a dispenser, which hung from the wall. He filled it twice with water and then drank it. He then took a seat on the ledge of the tub. He sat there until he felt he was okay to go back out and join the conversation. Dylan looked at himself in the mirror one last time, before exiting the bathroom.

Dylan made his way back to the living room area. Once he reached the end of the hallway he could already see that India and his brother were not where he had left them. "Hello! I'm back!" he yelled out. He waited, but still no reply. " Where the hell did they go?" Dylan whispered to himself as he continued to look around. He walked back towards the pool area and slid the glass door open. He peeked his head out, so he could look around, still there was no sign of them.

He reached his hand into his pocket in search of his car keys. He still had his keys, so he knew they had to be in the house. There were only two other places they could be. In the basement, or upstairs. Although India had declined to give them a tour of upstairs, Dylan had this funny feeling that that's exactly where he would find them. He walked towards the steps. "Ryan! India!" He called out once more, before climbing the steps. Still there was no response.

Once he reached the top, he stopped to catch his breath. All the beers he had drunk left him feeling winded. The Upper part of the house split into three directions. Dylan wanted to go right, but the door straight ahead of him was much larger than the others, also it was a totally different color from the others. This had to be India's bedroom. Dylan walked towards the door, still calling out their names, but still he heard nothing in return.

Before he twisted the knob to the door, he put his ear against it, to see if he could hear anything. Still he heard nothing. Dylan gently placed his hand over the doorknob and turned it. As the door opened he could see his brother standing up completely nude. India was in her bra and panties, down on her knees sucking his dick. Dylan could not believe what he was seeing. He wasn't sure if he should leave them be, or speak up, but at the moment one thing was for sure. He wanted to watch.

Both Ryan and India had their eyes closed. India had Ryan's entire penis drenched in her Saliva. There was not a part of his penis left unattended. Even his nut sack was moistened. She sucked his penis with such care, and passion. Dylan could feel his own stiffening just from watching. Dylan was about to leave them be, but India opened her eyes and spotted him looking in. She didn't look shocked to see him standing there. Not one bit. Instead she motioned for him to come in with her free hand.

Dylan stood there in disbelief. Ryan still hadn't opened his eyes. If Dylan were in his shoes he probably wouldn't have opened his eyes either. Dylan Nervously walked into the room. He didn't know what the hell to expect let alone what to do. As he got closer Ryan opened his a bit and then closed them slowly. Dylan could tell that he was really intoxicated, for one he was quiet, something that is rare for his twin brother, very rare. Surprisingly Dylan didn't have to make any decisions.

Once he had gotten close enough to India she began to undo his pants, while sucking Ryan's penis, and maintaining her rhythm and pace. Dylan's eyes wondered around the room as she undressed him. It was gigantic. The Room was an oval shape. India had a huge round bed right in the center of the room. Directly behind it was a huge window with long thick black curtains that you couldn't see out of.

To Dylan's right there were two huge wooden doors with glass squares that you could see through. Beyond the doors he could see a small balcony, which over looked the swimming pool. There was this opening in the corner that Dylan could not see inside of; it had to either be a walk in closet, a bathroom or both. To Dylan's left there was again another large window. This window was floor to ceiling. In front of it sat an antique looking chase. In the far corner there was a vanity set that matched the style of the chase.

Dylan was quickly snatched from his thoughts and back to reality, once his felt the warmth and wetness from India's mouth around the head of his penis. Dylan couldn't believe that this was actually her mouth giving him this pleasure. The way she gripped his penis felt just as good as it had looked moments ago. Dylan closed his eyes and put his head back towards the ceiling. The same look his brother once had a few minutes ago, Dylan now had that same identical look.

He held his shirt up, so that it would stay out of the way. India went back and forth between the two of them. She did not miss a beat. Dylan finally opened his eyes again and looked down. India's big brown eyes stared back at his. He almost felt ashamed for watching, but why should he. She was willing sucking him and his brother's dick. It was hard not to watch. In fact it seemed as though she enjoyed him watching, which was such a freaking turn on.

India took his penis deep into her mouth, until she started to gag on it. She then stroked it slowly with her lips, gently pulling back and forth. As she was taking him into her mouth again Dylan could feel himself climaxing. The way India's lips gripped the shaft of his penis; he had no choice but to cum in her mouth. The veins on his penis throb as his cum squirted out and filled the back of her throat. She continued to suck until he was done.

India slowly removed her lips. Some left behind semen from the head of his penis dripped from her bottom lip. India bit down on her lip sucking it up in the process. Dylan looked over at his brother. Ryan had already climaxed as well. His semen dripped from India's right hand. She shot a side look at Ryan, and then she grinned up at him. Ryan looked away, slightly embarrassed that she was able make him climax with just a hand job and oral sex.

"Excuse me," India said getting up and disappearing into the dark opening, which turned out to be both a walk in closet, and bathroom. Just as Dylan had expected. As Soon as they heard a door close Dylan reached down, and pulled his pants up. Dylan turned and whispered to his brother. "What the fuck Ryan. How did you guys get up here? How did you end up like this?" Dylan made a gesture with his hand at his brother's nudity.

Ryan looked over his shoulder before speaking. "Well we were talking, and I asked again if I could see the bedroom. We got up here and one thing lead to another, next thing I know I was butt naked getting some of the best head of my life." They both erupted with laughter. " Ryan quickly put his finger over his mouth to hush his brother up. "Man I think she's coming back. Play it cool. Don't mess this up with your nerdy niceness crap." Said Ryan.

Dylan screwed up his face at his brother's insulting remark. As Ryan was looking around for his clothing India came back in to the room. She was still in her bra and panties. She looked at both Dylan and Ryan, as she wiped her hand with a warm rag. " You guys going somewhere? Because I'm not done playing yet." Dylan and Ryan both looked at each other. Both of them shook their heads no. "Good! Get undressed then, and hand me your clothes." India said directing her attention more so towards Dylan since he was still clothed.

Dylan calmly took his clothes off and tossed them over to her. He smiled boyishly revealing those dimples of his once again. India shivered. She was enticed by Ryan's bad boy act, but it was something about Dylan's sweet, shy, behavior that took her mind back to high school days. Dylan simply made her melt. However the real satisfaction came from the fact, that she was able to explore and enjoy the both of them.

Now that India had gotten them warmed up. She didn't know exactly where she wanted to start, so she did whatever came to her mind first. She walked right up to Dylan and planted a big kiss on his lips. India wanted to do that ever since the time he shook her awake back at the club. She kissed him again, and again. Dylan kissed her back. When India felt satisfied she stepped back. She looked over at Ryan who stood patiently rubbing both his hands together.

India walked over to Ryan and grabbed the back of his neck, pulling his lips to hers. Ryan stuck his tongue in her mouth, kissing her back, while palming both of her ass cheeks. This kissed that they shared was rough yet passionate. India was so deeply wrapped up in her kiss with Ryan, so moved, her vagina began to get wet once again, and flow with juices. India continued to kiss Ryan, but used one of her arms to gesture to Dylan to join in.

Dylan gladly did so. He walked up behind India, and put his hands between her legs. Her Lace panties were still damp from her reaching her own climax, while sucking both of their dicks. Dylan kissed, and sucked her back, and neck. Ryan continued kissing her; squeezing her breast, ass, and whatever else he could get his hands on. India Gripped Ryan's Penis, then she reached back and gripped Dylan's as well. She Caressed, and jerked both of them gently.

India was extremely satisfied with the size of their penises, despite them both being so young. India let both of them kiss and get to know her body for a few more minutes. Then the three of them began to make their way to the bed. She told Dylan to lie back on the bed. India could tell by the way he kissed her that he was a gentle lover, and would last longer. Ryan on the other hand was rough, and straight to the point.

Therefore India preferred to fuck Dylan first. If she did things this way, she could cum a few times herself, and then let Ryan fuck her until she couldn't take anymore. With this in mind India stood over Dylan backwards. She instructed Ryan to stand up on the bed as well. India slowly lowered herself onto Dylan's hard penis, breathing deeply as she felt him entering her. "Mmm mmm," She let some of her moans escape, before they became muffled by Ryan's penis, entering her mouth.

Dylan gripped her waist from behind, as he pushed his entire dick inside of her. Ryan placed his hand behind India's Head gripping a handful of her hair. He pushed his penis in, and out of her mouth, each time going a little deeper, he found a rhythm and kept it going. Ryan didn't stop. Even though he could see India's eyes beginning to water. Still India held her ground, daring him to push further. This completely blew Ryan's mind.

India at that very moment made Ryan forget about any other female that had ever performed oral sex for him before her, point blank period. India continued to moan and deep throat his penis, while still going up, and down on Dylan's dick. Dylan held on to her shoulders pumping upward into her, making India cum again for the second time. Her juices seeped down her thighs, all over Dylan, and right on to the bed sheets.

"You like sucking my dick?" Ryan asked India softly, not wanting his brother to hear him. She moaned, and shook her head yes. "Awe shit" Ryan said aloud, while fucking her mouth slowly. He could feel himself about to give into her again, but not before He felt her on the inside. Ryan pulled back. "Its my turn." He moved his index finger in a circular motion, indicating that he wanted her to get on all fours. India was much obliged.

She reached down and pulled Dylan's hard dick out of her. She turned around on all fours. Dylan now stood up on the bed. He held his penis in his hand, as he guided it into India's mouth. India could taste a mixture of her own cum and his on her taste buds. She savored the taste. She could feel Ryan entering her from behind, with a lot of force, causing her to grip the bed sheets tightly. Ryan pulled her hair forcing her to feel his every stroke.

Him being so aggressive was also causing Dylan to have to move forward as well. Ryan put one of his hands on her shoulders. He stroked in, and out of her fast, and hard. Sweat fell from his body on to hers. Ryan put his head back and closed his eyes. He loved the way her pussy opened up each time he pushed deeper. It excited him even more when she clenched tighter each time he pulled backwards. Ryan wanted to say something. Nothing in particular, but something, just not while his brother could hear, so he refrained.

Instead he moved his hand from her shoulder, and angled his body slightly to the side, as he continued to stroke her insides. Ryan watched the head of his penis go in and out of her vagina opening. Ryan bit down on his lip and smacked India's ass cheeks. He dug his hands into the sides of her waist. Ryan could feel himself about to release his semen any moment, so he pumped harder. Right before he came he pushed her away, pulling his hard penis out quickly. By doing so he caused India's body to move, and instead of Dylan's semen making it into her mouth it squirted all over her breast, and chin instead.

Ryan didn't seem to care. He jerked the rest of his semen out on to her ass and back. Without warning he missed the bed, and ended up falling back on to the floor. He didn't even bother to pick himself up. Even if he wanted too he couldn't. He was too spent. Within seconds he was snoring loudly. Dylan and India laughed. "Wait right here. I'll grab you a wet cloth to clean yourself up." Dylan disappeared into the bathroom.

As he stood at the bathroom sink soaping up the rag he couldn't help but smile. He really just had sex with a woman more than 10 years older than him. And she was fine as hell, and not only did he get lucky, but his twin did too. Dylan turned the water off and returned to the bed. He helped India clean herself up. " Thank You" She said softly kissing his hand. " No thank you!" He said planting a kiss to her forehead.

CHAPTER TEN

BQE

"Now you know damn well we should not have another bottle of wine sent over," Dale said to his wife Jahaun as soon as the waiter left their table. Jahaun leaned over the table and motioned for Dale to come closer with her index finger. Once he was close enough she leaned in, and kissed his forehead, then his nose, followed by his lips. Jahaun picked her husband's glass up and placed it to his lips.

"Drink with me honey. Please. Just tonight. We can leave the car parked and come for it in the morning. Please! You know you want too." Jahaun pouted a bit. "Don't make me beg! But if I have too," She whispered into his ear with a devilish grin. "I will," She began to slowly nibble on his earlobe. Dale took the glass from her hands and slowly took a sip. He was taking his time to give her a definite answer. Even though they both already knew she had won.

Nevertheless Dale still wanted to show that he was running things. "Honey I don't know if I want to leave the car parked in some garage all night. You know the hourly rate for just one…" Jahaun raised her finger, and placed it over his lips, cutting him off. "I'll keep my heels on and the lights," She whispered into his ear. Dale couldn't help but smile at the thought of his wife's flawless legs wrapped around his neck, while his dick was deep inside her.

She already had him. Dale was down to stay, but he still wanted to act all manly. " You were going to keep your heels on regardless, because I said so!" " Oh is that so Mr.!" Jahaun said playfully. "You damn right," Dale said while slipping his hand behind her neck and pulling her close. He kissed her neck, and was about to begin sucking on it, when the waiter cleared his throat. Your Bottle Mr. and Mrs. Wright. They both looked up like teenagers caught in the act.

" Thank you," Dale said motioning for him to sit the bottle down. Jahaun quickly reached over, and fixed Dale's tie, as they parted a little. "See look at you, making us look all inappropriate in public." Dale said grinning in his wife's direction. Jahaun started laughing "Okay so blame it all on me Mr. Wright!" Dale grabbed the bottle of wine and poured them both another glass. Jahaun immediately raised her glass to propose a toast.

Dale chuckled at her. Jahaun always made a big deal out of the little moments, which is one of the reasons why he loved her. She always knew how to make him feel appreciated. " I just wanted to say that I love you so much and I'm happy that I found you. That is all!" Dale laughed, "I think that's the shortest toast you have ever made honey." He leaned in and planted a wet kisses on her lips "I love you more, and more, and more."

They raised their wine glasses and began to sip. About an hour or so had past. Dale and Jahaun were still at the restaurant enjoying themselves. Dale looked at his wife, without exchanging any words with one other, Jahaun began to gather her things, while Dale took care of the bill. Jahaun already knew that look. No words were necessary. Dale walked around the table to help her put on her long trench coat, then he slipped his on, wrapping his arm around Jahaun's waist as they exited.

They giggled and touched all over one another like newlyweds. Jahaun stumbled a bit. She leaned on Dale for support. "Easy Mrs. Wright don't break a heel. You're going to need them later on tonight." He winked at her. "Silly man," she said laughing at his sly remark. "How are we getting home though honey?" Jahaun looked around clueless. Dale laughed, "Oh so now I should have the answers. This was your bright ideal to leave my brand new car parked in some lot!" "Oh hush, did you have to add that it was brand new Dale?" Jahaun lightly tapped him on the arm. Dale grinned, "Indeed I did."

"Let's catch a cab. I can not stand to deal with mass transit at these hours." Jahaun said, while walking out into the street to hail a taxi. A yellow cab immediately stopped short in front of her and they hopped in. Dale gave the driver directions to their home. "Sir you can take the Brooklyn queens expressway it's much faster." Dale added in, as he sat back in the seat. Jahaun immediately began touching all over him. She sucked, and kissed all over his face neck, and lips.

The scent from her perfume and shampoo invaded Dale's nostrils. It amazed him, that after all these years her perfume still turned him on. He could feel his penis starting to harden. "Easy woman," he said grasping Jahaun's hands, which were slowly slipping lower, and lower. "Don't start something you know we can't finish at the moment." Jahaun frowned, while pushing Dale back into his seat. She straddled him, "I've never been one to start anything and not finish!" She reached down and gripped his penis. "And you should know that!" She added.

"Woman we are not about to do anything in this taxi! I'm not having this man see what's just for me!" Dale attempted to push her off his lap. Jahaun laughed, "Honey that man is not thinking about us! Besides as long as this trench coat is he won't be able to see anything anyways." Before Dale could say anything else she started nibbling on his earlobe, while massaging his spot with her tongue. Jahaun knew that got to him each and every time.

She slowly began to unzip his slacks and started to work her way down. Dale could already see what she was trying to do. He tried to grab a hold to her arms, as an attempt to stop her, but Jahaun was too quick. She slipped down to her knees, and took his dick into her mouth. He gave her a look of disapproval, which she totally ignored. Instead she winked at him as she took more of his penis into her mouth.

Dale Glanced at the driver to make sure that his eyes were on the road like they should be. He returned his attention back to his wife, who was now making love to his penis with her mouth. Dale could hear her moaning, as her head bobbed up and down. Dale put his head back, letting his eyes roll back in his head. He loved when she moaned while sucking his dick. Jahaun had the sexiest high pitch moan ever. Jahaun removed his penis from her mouth and smacked it against her tongue, then she licked around the shaft of it, as if she was licking one of those huge round rainbow colored lollipops.

Dale sat up to watch his wife. Jahaun smiled up at him with her eyes. She loved when he watched her pleasure him. Jahaun licked around the head of his thick penis. She then put it back into her mouth, and then she quickly pulled it out, making a smacking sort of slurping sound as she did so. Jahaun quickly put it back into her mouth once more. This time she inched every inch of it down her throat. Jahaun took her hand and began to jerk his penis, as she sucked. Jahaun could taste Dale's pre-cum on her taste buds, sending an indication that he was almost ready to climax.

Jahaun stuck her tongue in between the meatus of his penis, and began to suck hard. "Fuck, ahh shit, that's it! That's it," Dale said, as he looked down at her, his dick still appearing, and then disappearing between her juicy cherry colored lips. Dale grabbed a handful of her hair. Jahaun quickened the pace of the hand she was jerking with, and sucked the head of his dick, until she could feel his seamen hitting the sides of her cheeks. Dale held on to the back of her head, as if he was on a crazy roller coaster ride, or something of that nature.

Jahaun sucked every bit of his seamen out, and then swallowed it. She looked up at her husband, flashing him a smile, while wiping her mouth with her hand. She resembled a vampire, or animal like creature after draining blood from their prey. This gave Dale another hard on. Dale enjoyed when his wife did nasty acts for him. It wasn't just the fact that she did them, but she wasn't afraid to let him know that she enjoyed doing them for him.

Dale wanted to return the favor by eating her pussy,

until she called his name at the top of her lungs. But Dale knew there was no way in hell, that his tall frame could maneuver her into a pussy eating position, in the back seat of the taxi. Dale reached out his hand, using it to help pull Jahaun up from her knees. He was about to push her back into the seat, when she pushed him off of her. " Not tonight sir! I'm the captain of this ship Mr!" She pushed him over, so they wouldn't be in the way of the rearview mirror too much.

Jahaun straddle him once more. She opened her trench coat up all the way, and pushed it back, letting it drape over Dale's legs. She bent down and kissed her husband, sticking her tongue in his mouth, and sucking on his bottom lip. Dale ran his hands up her thighs, pulling her skirt up with his thumbs at the same time. He pulled her silk panties to the side, then ran his fingers along her clean-shaven pussy lips. They were so nice and plump; he couldn't resist squeezing them in-between his fingertips. He then spread them, and slid his index finger in. Once it was covered in Jahaun's pussy juices he removed it.

Dale brought his finger up to his mouth and sucked it, savoring the taste. "More please," He whispered, up to her. But Jahaun shook her head no. She wasn't having it. She knew if she let him taste more, then he would definitely take control of the situation. "Later," She said pushing his hands away. Jahaun reached down and guided his dick in the direction of her pussy. She moved the thick head of it back and forth, between her lips, and vaginal opening.

Once his penis was remoistened she eased herself down on it, punching her fits into the seat, as she felt all of him entering her. Dale grabbed her neck, and began kissing, and sucking all over it. He began to fidget with the small buttons of her white blouse. He quickly became frustrated. Dale took his hands, and yanked her blouse open, sending the buttons scattering all over the back seat. "I'll buy you a new one honey. I'll buy you a new one," He whispered, to her as he took one of her breast into his mouth.

Dale sucked on one of her breast, then the other, biting them, and leaving marks all over her. Jahaun pushed her hands up to the ceiling of the cab for support, as she stood up to bounce on her husband's dick. She went up and down slowly, while working her hips. She looked down at her husband. The facial expressions he was making fueled her even more. Just the thought of her being the only woman to please him, and ride his dick the way she was riding it, at that moment. It made her feel ways she couldn't even begin to explain.

Jahaun put her head back, letting herself cum all over his midsection for at least the third time. Jahaun was in her own little world. Dale on the other hand was enjoying it as well. Even though he was a control freak, Dale loved for his wife to take control sometimes. His wife's slow grinding was bringing him to yet another climax, but he wasn't ready to stop yet. Dale needed to penetrate her with more force before he gave in.

Dale put his hand around her neck, then wrapped his arm around her back, so she would have some type of support. He leaned her back a bit, while he thrusted his pelvis. He pushed deeper and harder inside her. Dale thrusted so hard the back of Jahaun's head began to bang against the partition slightly. Jahaun started to moan louder. She bit down on his forearm, as an attempt to muffle her moans. Dale repositioned himself, so that he could lean back a bit.

He pulled his slacks down some more. He grabbed a hold of Jahaun's shoulders, using them to pull her downward with as much force as he could. For a moment he couldn't see or hear anything, just the sound of her thighs slapping against his midsection, and her moaning that she would never leave him in his ear. Dale pushed up into her wet pussy as hard as he could one last time, then he gave in.

His penis jerked one last time, before his seamen shot out inside of her. The two of them sat there on top of each other in complete bliss, painting, kissing, and whispering I love you. They were so busy wrapped up in sweet nothings that they hadn't even noticed that the taxi had stopped moving. All the windows were fogged up. They couldn't even see out. The cab driver was gone. "Honey oh my gosh! We are not moving!" Jahaun said falling off his lap, trying to button her blouse, which had no buttons to button.

Dale quickly slipped his slacks up. If this cabbie had gone to call the authorities, the last thing he wanted to do was get caught with his pants down. As he leaned back to pull his slacks up over his ass, he noticed a crumpled up note attached to the partition that read: did not want to disturb. $46.50 is the fair. Dale began to laugh hysterically. Jahaun looked at him as if he had lost his mind. "And just what the hell is so funny?" She asked.

Dale pointed in the direction of the note. Jahaun read it out loud and started to laugh with him. Dale pulled his wallet out and pulled out a crisp bill. He slipped the hundred-dollar bill through the partition glass. "Honey I think you need to throw in a little more. This cab driver should have called the cops on our Asses!" Said Jahaun, buttoning her trench coat. "I think you're right honey we did get carried away. He peeled off another hundred and slipped it through the partition as well.

"Now let's go before he has a change of heart," Dale said. He opened the car door, and got out. "Hey wait for me!" Jahaun yelled after him. "You better shake a leg because I'm not bailing you out!" He laughed. Jahaun caught up to him right before he put the code in to open the gate. "Honey that was so much fun," She said in a drunk slur. "Indeed it was, I just can't understand how the hell we got home so fast!" Jahaun laughed, "Because it was your genius idea to take the BQE!"

CHAPTER ELEVEN

Sentimental Mood

Blair laid in her bra and panties, slumped across her window seat. Her clothes lay in a pile soaked and wet near her apartment door. In her hand she held a full glass of wine. What was left of the half empty bottle sat on the carpet below her. Blair had some candle melts being warmed in the distance by some tea lights. Her whole apartment smelt of passion fruit. Duke Ellington's in a sentimental mood played from her Bluetooth speakers, which were set up throughout her apartment.

Needless to say his piece echoed between the walls, making not just her soul sway and swirl like she was a dancer In the 30's. But for certain anyone within earshot of her place pulse was sure to be dancing. Blair sat up a bit, so that she could take a sip from her glass. She pushed her damp short hair away from her eyes and out of the way. She took a small sip, and then one huge gulp. Blair balanced the wine glass in one hand, while she leaned over, and felt around for the wine bottle.

Just as her hand had connected with the handle, a loud

strike of thunder exploded in the sky, causing her to jump back, spilling her drink slightly. "Got damn it!" Blair said aloud, while shaking some of the wine off her hand. She dipped her fingers into her mouth and slurped up a few drops. More so out of habit than anything, because she could have simply let the blanket underneath her catch them. Blair refilled her glass and then sat up straight.

She pressed her face up against the huge window glass, squinting her eyes to see out into the night sky. It was pouring down raining. It had been raining off and on all day. It just so happens that the one day she forgets her umbrella it decides to rain. Not just some light rain showers, but the sky decided to open up with lighting, thunder, and clouds. The works. Blair shook her head, and then ran her hands through her damp hair.

Had her, and Chad ended their little fall out only 10 minutes before she stormed out of his place. She would have made it home safe and dry. "Whelp at least I ended up with one out of the two." She said, as she sipped some more wine. Blair then hit repeat on the stereo remote. Blair pulled the blanket up over her shoulders and just sat there. She couldn't believe all that had happen in the past few weeks, days, and hours between her, and her boyfriend Chad. They had been arguing for the past four hours.

She had been trying to get him to see that she could no longer be with him, for reasons she couldn't explain to him, at least not without breaking his heart. This she knew and he just didn't understand that. But Chad continued to press the issue. He just wasn't trying to hear it. He had been begging and pleading for more of a concrete explanation, on why she wanted to throw in the towel on their five year relationship. An explanation other than she couldn't deal. Something other than she needed time, something more than she didn't want to hurt him. Something better than a bullshit it's me not you.

As much as Blair hated to admit it, He was absolutely in the right. He deserved an explanation. A damn good one, but most of all he deserved the truth. Something Blair didn't have the heart to deliver to him. *She wished that things were different. She wished that she didn't have to let him go. But most of all she wished she didn't have to choose.* Soon after that last thought began floating around in her brain her cell phone flickered, indicating that she had a new message. She reached over, and unlocked her phone.

The message read. *This very minute marks exactly 72 hours since I've last seen you. Missing you insane sexy lady, till I see you again... Sebastian.* Blair smiled. She was about to respond, but then decided against it. She knew if she did he would want her to meet him somewhere. Between the liquor, and the way she was feeling at the moment, she knew exactly how her night would end with him.

Blair didn't mind going that route. But she really didn't want to go that route. At least not while she still had Chad on her back about their broken relationship. Truth be told stepping out on him hurt her more than she could have ever imagined. Despite her unhappiness, and the fact that he hadn't yet given her the type of commitment that she wanted. He was actually a great guy. He was a hopeless romantic just like her, handsome, and once upon a time she actually was completely happy with him. But most importantly, once upon a time she was entirely happy with them.

Now here she was being dishonest, and making someone who actually gave a shit about her feel unworthy.

Blair could feel herself beginning to cry. She quickly dabbed at her eyes and then chugged down some more wine. *As much as she tried to act so unbothered and unaffected, the truth was really eating her up inside. Was she making a mistake letting go of Chad? Was she wrong for falling for all the things Sebastian offered? All the things that Chad had stopped doing, or refused to give her. Should she feel this bad?*

Right when another thought was about to pop into her head she heard two heavy knocks at her front door. Blair thought she was hearing things. She lowered the volume to the stereo and listened again. She had to make sure the wine hadn't consumed her too much. Sure enough within moments the heavy knocks came again. This time much more urgent. Nervously she stood up and walked in the direction of the door.

She stood on her tippy toes, so that she could see out of the peephole. Blair got a glimpse of Chad pacing back and forth. She quickly debated on whether or not she should let him in. Suddenly Blair had a flash back of the last episode Chad put on, when she decided she wasn't going to open the door for him. Chad not only woke up all her neighbors with his screaming, and banging at her door, but he was also almost taken away in handcuffs.

Blair sighed. She didn't need that. Definitely not right now. Blair took a deep Breath Before Taking the Chain off the door. She didn't even bother waiting until Chad fully stepped foot through the door. She opened it just enough for him to get in, then she turned around, and walked back towards her spot by the window. Blair sat down, and continued to sip from her wine glass. She could hear Chad taking off his wet sneakers in the distance. She took a deep breath, as an attempt to try to brace herself for round two of his raft of anger, hurt, and pleading.

Blair could See Chad's reflection in the window clearly. He was taking a seat across the room at the other window seat. For a few moments they both sat in place not saying a word, letting Duke take them back to wonderful memories. Without warning Chad's Deep baritone broke the silence. "Come here." He said very firmly. Blair took her time guzzling down what was left in her glass, and then sat it down with a thump.

As much as she wanted to put up a fight she went against it. She heard the seriousness in Chad's voice, and knew he meant business. She got up off the cushion. Slowly she walked over to him. Blair stopped directly in front of him. Chad kept his head bowed for a few moments, as she stood there in front of him. He reached out for her waist, pulling her closer. Chad laid his head against her stomach. He then got down on his knees, and looked up at her.

"Tell me what you want me to do Blair, and I will do it! Am I not good enough for you? Please baby I love you; just tell me how I can fix this. Let me fix this. I don't want to lose you." Blair could feel the tears beginning to well up in her eyes. She looked up at the ceiling trying to avoid contact with his eyes as long as possible. She was afraid that he might see right through her. Blair took her hand, and ran it over his head of hair.

Chad usually kept a very short and neat cut, but his hair was thick & curly at the moment. This was probably due to him skipping a hair cut or two. Blair gripped a handful of strands in between her fingers, tugging them slightly, forcing Chad to look up at her. Blair took a deep breath. She then opened her eyes, and stared at him. The look that greeted her nearly broke her heart. Chad's amber colored eyes had a glossy look to them. He had bags under eyes, more than likely due to depriving himself of sleep.

Chad had always been a well-dressed man. This was one of the many things Blair loved about him. But tonight in that very instance he looked a messed. He looked completely distraught. Blair could literally see all the pain she had caused him. It made her feel like dreck, perhaps worst than dreck. She closed her eyes again, letting the hot tears flow freely down her face.

How could she break this mans heart by telling him that there was someone else? That someone other than him had been making her smile, laugh, and dance. How could she get up the nerve to tell him someone else had made her feel sexy? How could she look this man square in the eyes and tell him that she had been sleeping with someone else? Or better yet that someone else had been pleasuring her body, making her cream 2-3 times a week when possible.

How could she reveal that in her free time she daydreamed about another mans penis, penetrating her pussy walls until she screamed for him to stop? How could she basically sum up to him that she is a low down, dirty, lair? Who has carried herself like someone with no morals or respect for him, or herself for that matter. Lastly how could she reveal to him that she's not the good woman that he thinks she is? How could she let those words slip off her tongue, and escape her lips?

Blair's thought raced, until she began to tremble. She slowly slid down to the floor next to Chad. He wrapped his arms around her ever so tightly. "Shhh," He whispered in her ear. Trying to soothe her. "Tell me. Whatever it is baby we can fix it. I swear I only want you." Blair closed her eyes tighter. She had to tell him the truth no matter

4 Head Kissers Short Erotic Tales

how much she knew it would hurt him. She took a deep breath, as she continued to shake, and cry.

Through her sobs she managed to make out, "I've been sleeping with someone else." The words slowly left her lips, putting her mind at ease, while on the other hand hitting Chad right in the face, like a ton of bricks. Chad could feel his grip tightening around Blair, when she began to squirm he snapped back to reality. He was profoundly hurt, he felt betrayed, and foolish. Chad had been nothing but good to this woman, and here she was telling him, that she had been sleeping with someone else.

Chad really wanted to choke the living shit out of her, but instead he pulled her head to his chest. He whispered to her in a horse raspy tone. "Did you use protection?" Blair stop sobbing long enough to mouthed a yes to him. "Every time?" He asked, gripping, and shaking her aggressively. "Got damn it Chad! I used it every single time!" Blair said, raising her voice, and then lowering it quickly. "I know this means absolutely nothing, but I'm sorry. Please don't hate me. If Only I..."

"Just shut up Blair! Just shut the fuck up!" Chad said cutting her off. He took his hand, and gripped her face between it tightly. He wanted to put her head through the damn window. Instead he pulled her face to his, he kissed her rough, and passionately. Chad could still taste the liquor she had been consuming moments earlier on her tongue and lips. Blair got up a bit. She straddled him, wrapping her legs around his back, running her hands over his head, while they held their lip lock.

Chad's hands roamed all over Blair's body. A body he hadn't caressed in almost three long months. As much as he hated to admit, Blair's body felt so good in his arms at

132

that moment, even if she was a lying cheating piece of shit. He unsnapped her bra letting her breast free. They continued to kiss wildly. He could feel her pierced nipples through his wet t-shirt. Blair reached down, pulling at the ends of his shirt. Basically giving him the heads up to lift his arms up, which he gladly did, letting her pull his shirt over his head.

They parted briefly, and then began kissing, sucking, and tonguing each other down. Chad fondled her breast, pinching, and squeezing her hard nipples between his thumb, and index fingers. Without warning he gripped the back of Blair's neck, pulling her lips away from his. He pushed her backwards forcing her to bend as though she were playing limbo. Chad bent forward with her. He took one of her breast into his mouth. He sucked on it gently at first, letting her nipple ring bars hit against the tip of his tongue.

Chad then applied pressure with his teeth, causing Blair to moan out loud. "Oh my gosh Chad." He could hear her whispering faintly. Chad's Dick was bulging through his wet sweatpants. Between him sucking Blair's perfect shaped nipples, her moaning his name, and dry humping his midsection. It seemed as though his dick was getting harder, and harder by the second. Chad pulled Blair's panties to the side, and slid one of his fingers into her wet pussy.

Her fat vagina lips covered his fingers right away. He didn't even have to work his fingers in and out of her, because Blair reached down, and guided them in, and out for him. Chad removed his hand, and placed it face down on the floor, using it as a brace to help him stand up. He griped Blair's back tightly as he stood up, and walked over to the window seat. Chad violently pulled at the blanket that laid across it, quickly throwing it down to the floor, and laying Blair on top of it.

He reached down, and yanked at her underwear, ripping them completely off. Chad then pulled his sweatpants, and briefs down to his ankles. He pulled them down so quickly it caused his stiff dick to swing from left to right in mid air, and then it landed between his thighs curving slightly to the right. Chad reached down and gripped his dick firmly, as he inched his way down to the floor, on top of Blair.

He grabbed one of her legs, putting it over his shoulder, as he pushed his dick inside of her warm pussy. He could see her cum beginning to moisten, and drench the entire shaft of his dick. Chad pulled back slightly, running his hand over his dick, then he pushed it right back in. Chad grabbed a hold of both her legs, pushing them way behind her, pinning them as far back as they could go. Chad Slammed in and out of her, not caring one bit how loud Blair's screams became.

He pushed deeper and deeper, spreading her legs open wider. Blair dug her nails into Chad's back, and butt cheeks, encouraging him to go on, as she continued to moan loudly. Chad's entire's body was overcome with perspiration, and so was Blair's. Chad quickly got down to the floor, and laid on his back. He begin tugging, and pulling at his ankles, trying to get his sweatpants completely off.

Blair took this as her chance to take control. She mounted Chad taking his entire dick inside of her. She got on to her feet a little, and bounced up and down on his dick, biting her lip, and squeezing her breast as she did so.

Blair looked Chad in his eyes, but he quickly looked away. He tapped Blair's shoulder, indicating to her that he wanted her to turn around. She obliged without even getting up. Blair just reversed on top of him, while his dick still throbbed inside of her.

Chad sat up, and rubbed his hand down her spine. He then took her damp hair, and wrapped it around his free hand. As Blair rode him backwards he applied extra penetration, by pulling her hair each time she backed up. Blair's mouth was wide open yelling out things Chad couldn't quite make out. He let go of her hair, and leaned forward, griping her front body securely, as he walked over to the huge windows again. Chad pressed Blair's body up against the window, while he continued to penetrate her pussy from behind.

Both of their Shadows Glistened under the candlelight, leaving a huge shadow across the floors, and outside the rain continued to fall hard. Chad could feel himself about to cum. He clenched Blair's Waist as tight as he could. He moved in, and out of her at a fast pace. Right before his cum shot out inside of her. He pulled out, letting it land all over her backside. Once he released himself he fell against Blair, who seemed to be glued to the window.

They both stood there panting frantically trying to catch their breath. Slowly they both made their way down to the blanket, which they had laid down on the floor earlier. Before Blair's head could hit Chad's Chest She was asleep. For a few moments Chad just laid there looking up at the ceiling, taking in all that just happened. Chad was still trying to wrap his mind around the news that Blair had been keeping from him.

He leaned down, and kissed Blair on her forehead. He

then gently wiggled from underneath her. He put his damp clothing back on in a hurry, and then he quickly blew out all of the candles Blair had lit. Chad grabbed his wet sneakers from the corner, opened the front door, carefully slipping out of it, and closing it behind him.

To be continued...

CHAPTER TWELVE
Coming Soon

Kb took a seat on one end of the couch, and unzipped his denim jeans. He loosened his belt, and pulled his jeans down to his mid thigh. Kb's hard penis lay stiff across his lap in his plaid boxers. The woman standing in front of him bent down, and planted soft kisses on his neck. Kb's homeboy Rod sat on the opposite end of the couch, with a different female who was entertaining him.

Kb was trying his hardest to block his friend out, and not focus on what he had going on. The female that was entertaining him, now whispered in his ear. "How about you get undress for me boss man," Kb felt a sudden qualm. He didn't like the idea of being naked in a room with his homeboy. His eyes darted quickly to the opposite end of the couch again. Kb saw that Rod was already in compliance with the female's friend, taking off his footwear, jewelry, and clothing.

"Oh so y'all into that freaking kinky shit huh? Threesomes and foursomes," he could hear Rod saying aloud. Rod looked over at Kb, and flashed a devilish grin.

He then nodded a look of approval in Kb's direction. Kb smiled faintly, and then directed his attention back towards the beautiful female in front of him. She was amazing. Her body, her face, the way she licked her lips, her seductive tone when she called him boss man, her soft touch, her skin, her smile, and the way she smelt. It was all so exotic. She was nothing short of perfect.

The thought of having her bent over the couch, or performing oral sex for him, while he held her hair back, brought a devilish grin to his face. The same devilish grin his friend Rod held only moments ago. Kb rubbed his hands together. "How about you get undressed for me beautiful, then come do something with this." Kb licked his lips, and then grasped his erect penis.

"Anything for you boss man." She bent down, and planted kisses on Kb's neck once more, then whispered in his ear again. "But first I want you completely naked. I want to see all of you. Don't you want to feel my skin up against yours?" She asked, rubbing his face, and caressing his penis at the same time. Again Kb felt uneasy about getting undressed, but the temptation of having this beautiful female overpowered that feeling.

He began to take his jewelry off. He laid them on the table at the end of the couch. He removed his pistol from its holster. He then stood up, and undid his laces, slipping off his sneakers. Kb tucked his gun inside one of his sneakers. He then took off his hat and sweater, followed by his undershirt, jeans, and boxers. Kb threw them all into a pile on the floor near the couch. "Ok now beautiful, let me see what you have to offer underneath all this black.

Kb grinned sheepishly, while standing before her, his homeboy, and the other female completely in the nude.

"Not so fast!" She said, pushing him back down on to the couch. "What do you mean?" Kb asked, looking confused. "I want to do something for you first." She nodded in the direction of her female friend, who was in the process of trying to slow the pace down of Rod, who was groping all of her private areas.

Her friend peeled Rod's hands off of her, and then seductively walked over to the stereo system, turning it on. She skimmed the stations; until she found something slow enough to dance to. But loud enough so that the neighbors nor anyone else, would be able to hear what was going on inside. The two females began to slowly walk towards one another. Then they slowly began to dance, touch, and grind on each other. Kb and Rod slapped each other high fives, as they continued to look on in amazement.

The both of them were grinning from ear to ear. The females danced together for a few minutes more, then her friend walked back over to Rod, and she back over to Kb. She slid down on to Kb's lap, and whispered in his ear again. "Are you not entertained boss man?" All Kb could make out with his mouth was a deep slow, "Mmmm hmmm." He grabbed her butt, and sucked on her neck roughly. Kb reached in to undo her pants, but again she stopped him.

Confusion spread over Kb's face once more. He knew he was being teased now, and he was not feeling in control of the situation, what so ever. Kb did not like this feeling at all, now agitated he blurted out, "Are you going to do something with him or what?" He reached down, and stroked his erect penis, which stood straight up. She looked over at her friend, who was already performing oral sex on Rod, due to him being so impatient.

She Frowned, and then directed her attention back to Kb, easing down on to her knees, until she was in between his legs. The female then took her hands, and caressed Kb's penis, she licked her lips, and looked up at him as she did so. Kb stared back at her mesmerized, enthralled by her beauty, and the thought of the pleasure he was about to receive from her. She licked the shaft of his penis first. Then kissed the head of it, teasing him some more.

She removed her hands, and let her mouth do all the work. She wrapped her lips around the head of his penis, and sucked. She went up and down, until her spit had moistened his entire penis. She used her hands to caress, and massage his chest. Kb was on cloud nine, and shocked a little. He was still stunned at how beautiful she was. He couldn't believe that she was performing oral sex on him in exchange for nothing.

All he did was let her smoke some of his product, some marijuana, which she had paid for. It was almost too good to be true. He closed his eyes, and put his head back, allowing her to pleasure him blindly. This was one hell of a welcome to New York. She knew exactly what she was doing too. Her mouth felt warm, she held just the right grip, she used her tongue well, she kept a steady rhythm, and pace.

This female was sending this relaxing sensation all over his body. This was the best for him by far. The girls back home in Philly couldn't compare, at least not the ones that he had encountered. For a brief moment he seemed to have blacked out. Kb kept his eyes closed, and head back. He forgot about his homeboy on the opposite end of the couch. Kb forgot about being uneasy, and embarrassed.

He could no longer hear the music or anything else, it's like his entire body went numb. Nothing mattered at that moment, but the pleasure she was providing for him. He didn't even notice that she was slowing down, until she came to a complete stop. Kb heard Rod yell out, "Oh shit!" Kb's eyes popped wide open. He was starring down the barrel of a 45-caliber pistol. His heart felt as if it jumped right out of his chest.

His tongue felt as if it dried up completely. His penis fell limp between his legs. Kb's mind was scrambling to make out what was taking place. He reached for his pistol, but was stopped dead in his tracks. "Make one false move, and I promise you it will be your last. Hands up! This is a motherfucking stick up!"

Begging For More? Heres a sneak peek at some of the tittles for
4 head kissers volume II

Coming Soon

Beard Gang

Nulda Cane

Long ass Ride to baltimore

The Happy Ending (In a Sentimental Mood Part 2)

Just The Head

Stay tuned for more info and release dates at: www.4headkissres.com
Follow me on twitter at: @Monaejae4hk
Follow me on Instagrarm at : @monaejae

Monáe Jae

Like me on Facebook at: Monae Jae

Monae Jae Was Here …

www.ingramcontent.com/pod-product-compliance
Lightning Source LLC
Chambersburg PA
CBHW051250170626
46809CB00004B/1575